"You're Daniel ... who saved that b...

"Hardly a hero," Daniel said.

"I didn't know…" Leah hesitated. "Now I feel foolish. I spent so much time with you tonight and I never asked you about your travels. I really feel foolish."

"Don't. It was a natural mistake." He struggled to find the right thing to say. He didn't want her to walk away feeling embarrassed. "I'll be looking for you—at the presentation. I hope you aren't disappointed."

"*No*," Leah said. "You couldn't disappoint anyone, Daniel Brown. Least of all, me."

"I'll see you there, then?"

"Leah?" A woman called from the porch. "Are you ready?"

"*Ya*," she answered. "Coming." She smiled at him. "I'm glad you were with me tonight."

"Me, too."

"What you said before…" she murmured shyly. "I agree. We made a good team."

"We did," he said. And then, without another word, she turned and hurried off, leaving him standing there, staring after her and wishing she wasn't going.

Books by Emma Miller

Love Inspired

*Courting Ruth
*Miriam's Heart
*Anna's Gift
*Leah's Choice

*Hannah's Daughters

EMMA MILLER

lives quietly in her old farmhouse in rural Delaware amid fertile fields and lush woodlands. Fortunate enough to be born into a family of strong faith, she grew up on a dairy farm, surrounded by loving parents, siblings, grandparents, aunts, uncles and cousins. Emma was educated in local schools, and once taught in an Amish schoolhouse much like the one at Seven Poplars. When she's not caring for her large family, reading and writing are her favorite pastimes.

Leah's Choice
Emma Miller

Love Inspired

Recycling programs
for this product may
not exist in your area.

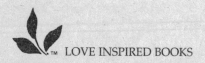 LOVE INSPIRED BOOKS

ISBN-13: 978-0-373-81620-0

LEAH'S CHOICE

www.LoveInspiredBooks.com

Printed in U.S.A.

Do not press me to leave you
Or to turn back from following you!
Where you go, I will go;
Where you lodge, I will lodge;
Your people shall be my people.
And your God my God.
—*Ruth* 1:16

Chapter One

Kent County, Delaware, Spring

More than forty people, Mennonite and Amish, waited in the old Grange building for the speaker's arrival. A long table covered with photographs and maps stood at the rear of the hall, and volunteers had arranged folding chairs in two sections, one on either side of a central aisle. Leah Yoder, three of her sisters, her brother-in-law, and nine giggling and whispering Amish teenagers from Seven Poplars filled the first two rows on the left.

It was rare for Old Order Amish to attend events hosted by other denominations, but tonight was an exception. Leah's older sister, Miriam, and her husband, Charley, had volunteered to chaperone the outing for their church's youth group, the Gleaners, and the bishop had given them special permission to do so. Leah, at twenty, was too old for the Gleaners, but she had been just as eager as her younger sisters, Rebecca and Susanna, to see the PowerPoint presentation and hear the Mennonite missionary share his experiences in spreading God's word outside the United States.

A young man in jeans and a raincoat, carrying a briefcase and a camera, wandered in from the offices in the back, and Leah thought that he might be the speaker, but it was only a reporter from a local newspaper. She hoped that he wouldn't attempt to take photos of the audience. Having pictures taken was against Amish beliefs, and if he tried to snap their picture, Charley and Miriam might decide that it was better to leave. To Leah's relief, the man found a seat near the front and didn't even look across the aisle at them.

The program had been scheduled to start at seven, but it was already twenty past the hour and Susanna was growing restless. Susanna had been born with Down syndrome, and although she was eighteen, in many ways, she would always be a child. Leah had convinced their mother to allow her to bring Susanna to the presentation this evening, so her sister was her responsibility.

Susanna wasn't the only one losing patience with the long wait. Herman Beachy, who could never sit still for long, was tugging at his sister Verna's bonnet strings and, by the expression on her face, she appeared ready to give him a sharp elbow in the ribs. Amish considered themselves nonviolent, but that didn't mean brothers and sisters didn't have their spats. Leah could see that the rest of the Gleaners were keyed up as well. If the youngsters became unruly, it would reflect badly on the entire Amish community, and that would put an end to any future outings of this kind.

Leah leaned forward, cleared her throat and threw Charley a meaningful look. *See what's keeping him,* she mouthed silently.

We'll just wait, he mouthed in return.

Leah rolled her eyes in exasperation. What was wrong with Charley? It had been his idea to bring the youth group, but now that they were here and things weren't going as smoothly as expected, her usually gregarious brother-in-law seemed unsure of himself. Even Miriam seemed out of her element.

Leah wished she and Rebecca had come alone, as she'd first planned when she'd seen the notice for Daniel Brown's talk. The sisters had recently returned to Delaware after spending a year in Ohio caring for their aging grandmother and great-aunt. The Amish church in *Grossmama*'s community had been more liberal than in Seven

Poplars, and she and her sister had often gone to dinners, charity auctions and programs put on by the Mennonites. There, the two denominations mingled more regularly than in Seven Poplars.

Leah had never stopped to think that not all Old Order Amish were so at ease with the Mennonite community. And the same went for the Mennonites. She'd certainly seen it tonight when the Amish had all taken seats on one side of the aisle and the Mennonites on the other. And now, both Charley and Miriam, of all people, seemed nervous. Well, if they wouldn't go see what was going on, she'd have to.

"Stay here with Rebecca," she whispered to Susanna as she stood up.

Smiling, Susanna nodded and clasped Rebecca's hand.

Leah crossed the aisle to where a gray-haired woman stood talking anxiously to a middle-aged man. Dinah was a cheerful woman who always wore a modest dress and a white crocheted head covering. She often stopped by the Yoder farm to purchase large quantities of eggs for her church bake sales. It was Dinah who'd made a special point of inviting the Seven Poplars Amish community to hear the speaker.

"It's an opportunity not to be missed," she'd said to Leah's mother, Hannah, a few weeks ago. "Daniel Brown faced down an angry Moroccan mob to rescue a homeless youth falsely accused of theft. If Daniel hadn't put his own life in danger to interfere, a tragedy could have occurred."

"An excellent role model for our children," Mam had agreed. She'd said no more about Daniel Brown, but Leah had seen her mother deep in conversation with their bishop after church the following Sunday. Both Leah and Miriam were convinced that it was due to Mam's powers of persuasion that Bishop Atlee had agreed that the Gleaners should accept the invitation to hear the young missionary speak.

But now they were here and anxious for the program to begin…and there was no Daniel Brown in sight.

"I apologize for the delay," Dinah said as Leah approached. "Daniel's on his way. He's usually very dependable, but he had some problem. Something about leaving his coat at a rest stop." Dinah chuckled. "Men. But, we're so pleased that so many from your church have come out to hear Daniel, especially the young people."

"We didn't want them to miss hearing Daniel's story," Leah said. "How often do we have a real hero in our midst?"

"Exactly," Dinah agreed. "Oh, Leah, do you know my eldest son, Raymond?" When Leah nodded, Dinah went on. "Raymond's been trying to reach Daniel on his cell phone to see how soon he expects to arrive, but he hasn't had any luck. We thought he'd be here by now."

"I'm sure it's just the storm." Leah offered a quick smile.

It was raining hard outside, and the wind was rattling the shutters. Earlier, as they'd driven here from the farm, they'd been caught in a sudden flurry of thunder and lightning so fierce that Leah had wondered if she should turn back, but that had passed, leaving just a steady downpour. Fortunately, there was a long, open shed with a good roof behind the Grange where they could shelter the horses and buggies.

"Daniel's driving up from Richmond," Dinah explained, "and I understand that Virginia's had bad weather all day."

The side door opened, and everyone glanced up expectantly. "Evening, Daniel," Dinah said. "Maude." The couple took seats on the Mennonite side in the last row, and Dinah turned back to Leah. "That's Daniel *Warner* and his wife." She dropped her voice to a whisper. "They're always late."

"I'd hoped that was the speaker," Leah said.

Dinah laughed. "We seem to have a lot of Daniels in our community. It's a popular name among us. One of my sons is also a Daniel. Named after my father-in-law. My husband always teased that perhaps we should give them nicknames to keep the Daniels straight." Another gust of wind shook the windowpanes and she grimaced. "If we'd realized that it would be such a nasty evening, we could have postponed until tomorrow night."

"I see that there are pictures and other material up front." Leah pointed. "I was wondering if it would be all right if the young people looked at them while we're waiting." She chuckled. "You know how impatient youngsters can get. They've been looking forward to tonight for weeks."

"Absolutely," Dinah said. "And we have a refreshment table. There's no reason we shouldn't all enjoy lemonade and cookies while—"

Abruptly, the heavy door at the front of the building banged open and a blast of wind blew through the hall sending photos and maps flying. Leah turned to see a tall, slim man about twenty-five years old standing in the doorway. Water dripped off his jean jacket and the bill of his ball cap, pooling on the floor. A gust tore at the door, threatening to wrench it out of his grasp, but he held it open until ten-year-old Abraham Beachy ducked into the hall.

Abraham was even wetter than the man in the jean jacket and ball cap. The Amish boy's face was pale and he looked frightened. The man said something to him that Leah couldn't hear, but Abraham just shuffled his feet and stared at the floor.

The newcomer looked up and cleared his throat. "Could I have your attention, please!" He nodded to Abraham who shook his head. "Go ahead," he urged.

Everyone in their chairs who hadn't turned around to look when they made their entrance, turned now.

Abraham swallowed hard and a deep flush rose from his throat to tint his face. "…Need help," he squeaked. "…Joey."

Charley stood up and hurried toward Abraham. "What's wrong?" he demanded.

Abraham, an undersized lad, burst into tears. Leah left Dinah and Raymond and walked down the aisle toward the Beachy boy.

"Abraham's parents—Norman and Lydia Beachy—have asked for help," the stranger said, speaking for Abraham. "It seems one of their children—"

"Joey!" Abraham wailed. "We can't…can't find…Joey."

"Their six-year-old son has gone missing," the man explained calmly, turning his attention to the Amish side of the aisle. "The family has asked if your youth group can come to their farm and help with the search."

Miriam walked up to the stranger. "Of course," she said. "We'll all help."

Chairs scraped against the worn floorboards. Everyone in the hall, Amish and Mennonite alike, stood.

"We have to look for Joey," Abraham managed. "It's all my fault. I…I lost him."

"It'll be all right." Miriam put an arm around Abraham. She was short, but Abraham's head barely reached her chin.

"Lost him where?" Leah asked. She couldn't imagine a six-year-old out in this weather. It didn't make sense. Maybe he was hiding somewhere in the rambling Beachy farmhouse or in the barn or outbuildings. With fourteen children under the age of sixteen, it was easy for Lydia to lose track of one little boy. That didn't mean that Joey was really lost.

Herman Beachy, Abraham's brother, hurried up to him. "What do you mean you *lost* him?" Herman demanded. Their sister, Verna, covered her face with her hands and sank back into her chair.

"How did you find out about the missing boy, Daniel?" A Mennonite girl only a little younger than Leah joined them. "Daniel's my cousin," she whispered to Leah. "I'm Caroline Steiner. I think you know some of my Steiner cousins in Ohio. From Hope Mennonite Church?"

"Sophie and Jeanine." Leah nodded.

"Hey, Caroline." Daniel offered a worried smile. "It's good to see you. Abraham's father flagged me down at the end of his lane," he explained. "He knew that some of the young people from their church were here with their group leaders and asked if I could bring Abraham to ask for help looking for the boy."

"You can count on us," Charley said.

He and Miriam went back to their group and began to organize them. Leah knew that some of the children were too young to join in. The girls' parents, especially, would want them safely delivered home. Luckily, they'd come in four buggies. Rebecca could be trusted to drive Susanna and some of the others home; Miriam could manage the rest.

As for Leah, she had no intention of going home. She'd always had a particular fondness for freckle-faced Joey. She would offer to take Verna, Abraham and Herman back to the Beachy farm, and once she was there, no one would object to her joining the search.

As the Amish moved toward the doors, the newcomer strode past Leah and called out to the Mennonites. "Michael? Gilbert? Who'll come with me to find the boy?"

"I'd be glad to," a stout man answered. "I've got a flashlight in the truck, but there are a lot of woods and fields around here, and I'm not familiar with the area."

"So we'll form groups," Daniel said, checking his pockets. "Someone can ride with me, if they like…soon as I find my keys." He looked up, extracting keys from a jacket pocket. "We'll make certain that there's someone in each group who does know their way." There was a chorus of agreement as men and women raised their hands and offered to help.

Leah knotted her bonnet strings and waved at Caroline just before dashing out into the rain. It made her feel good that Caroline's cousin had urged the others to join in the search.

She couldn't help but think how attractive the new Daniel was. He had a serious but handsome face, and nice hands that were never still when he was talking, even after he'd found his keys. As he'd walked past her in the aisle, Leah had noticed that his eyes were clear green—he had beautiful eyes. She couldn't remember ever meeting anyone with eyes that green before.

After telling the children to wait for her at the door, Leah made a run for the buggy. With so many more volunteers, she was certain they'd find Joey quickly. As Mam often said, most people had good hearts and were willing to do the right thing, if someone would just point them in the right direction.

* * *

Minutes later, Leah guided her horse up the muddy lane to the Beachy farmhouse. Buggies, SUVs and pickup trucks already filled the yard. Amish neighbors always came to help out in any emergency, but the Mennonites and Englishers were more than welcome. Norman, Joey's father, stood in the pouring rain, shaking hands with friends and strangers alike and thanking everyone for coming, but it was Samuel Mast, their church deacon, who appeared to be in charge.

One of the kids took Leah's horse and promised to find the mare a dry stall in the barn. A red-eyed Lydia came to the back door and called for Leah to join the women in the kitchen. Leah hesitated, then went in, but kept her green rain slicker on. It wasn't Amish clothing, but Mam had bought everyone in the family one at an Englisher store years ago.

"I'm going right back out," Leah explained to the worried Lydia. "To help with the search."

As usual, Lydia's kitchen was complete chaos, with toddlers dashing about, a cat carrying kittens to a basket in the corner of the room, and Jesse, Joey's twin brother, climbing up on the counter to get something out of the cupboard.

Leah was surprised to see her Aunt Martha standing at the counter making coffee. Aunt

Martha and Lydia didn't usually visit each other's homes, and Leah wondered how her aunt had heard the news about Joey and gotten here so fast, but then Leah's mother, Hannah, came from the hallway with Lydia's newest baby in her arms.

Samuel must have gone for Mam, Leah thought, leaving her sister Anna, his wife, home with their children. Samuel would have guessed that Lydia needed Hannah, Leah's mother. And somehow, Aunt Martha had included herself in the emergency.

"You're certain you want to go out with the men?" Aunt Martha asked. She had the misfortune to be born with a nasally voice that always came out sounding as if she was peeved at someone.

Leah nodded. "I am."

"I told you she would." Hannah handed the fussing baby to Lydia.

Aunt Martha wiped her hands on her apron, poured a cup of steaming coffee and pressed it into Leah's hands. "Drink this," she ordered. "If you're determined to go out in this rain and catch your death, you'll need it."

"Thanks, Aunt Martha, but I couldn't drink a drop."

Her aunt frowned, and Leah knew she'd offended her again when she voiced a *thank you*. Most Amish considered *please* and *thank you* to be fancy words. *Showing off.* The service to one another and the thanks were assumed, and such words weren't bandied about, but that was another habit she'd picked up from her more worldly friends back in Ohio.

"I need to go." Leah gave the coffee to her mother. "The search parties are getting organized."

"I wouldn't stand for my Dorcas to be out in the dark with strangers. Not my daughter," Aunt Martha fussed. "That's a man's place, not a woman's, and certainly not a girl's." She threw a meaningful look at Mam. "This is what comes of her running wild out in Ohio, going to fairs with her Mennonite friends, eating ice cream at all hours and taking herself to every frolic in the county."

"Not every frolic, Aunt Martha," Leah defended. "Rebecca and I spent most of the time taking care of *Grossmama*."

Aunt Martha scowled. "Not what I hear."

"All these years and all these blessed children, and I've lost nary a one before," Lydia fretted to no one in particular, rocking the baby. "Where can my Joey be?"

"*I'm* here, Mam," Jesse piped up.

"You hush," Lydia corrected. "And get down off that counter before I dust your bottom."

Jesse ignored her and kept digging in the cabinet. Aunt Martha scooped him up, deposited him on the floor and said. "You heard your mother. Shoo!"

Jesse shooed.

"Joey's just turned six and he's scared of the dark." Lydia glanced at the dark windows. "Where can he have got to?"

"We'll find him," Leah promised.

"Be glad you've got other children," Aunt Martha intoned as she cut herself a slice of chocolate cake. "Reuben and I were never so blessed."

Leah wished her aunt had stayed at home. Lydia didn't need to hear that. She was worried enough. "Have the kids searched the barns and the house?" Leah asked.

Lydia nodded. "Root cellar to attic. I've had the girls digging through the straw in the hayloft and looking under the chicken house. God help him, he's such a rascal to put us all through this."

Mam removed her blue headscarf and handed it to Leah. "Give me your *kapp* and bonnet," she said. "The woods at night are no place to be wearing your bonnet. And button up your slicker all the way. It will keep the rain off."

"Be quick about it," Aunt Martha said. "It's not seemly for either of you to go uncovered. With all these Englishers and Mennonites wandering about, no telling who might take it into his head to wander in the kitchen without knocking."

Leah quickly traded head coverings with her mother.

Seconds later, Charley opened the door and peered in. "Come on if you're coming, Leah. Samuel's assigning groups to search together."

"I've got to go, Mam." Leah gave the ends of the headscarf she tied beneath her chin a firm tug.

Fresh tears filled Lydia's eyes and rolled down her cheeks. "You find my Joey," she murmured, rocking the baby against her.

"I'll do my best," Leah said.

Her mother put her arms around Leah and kissed her on the forehead. "You take care, daughter. I'd not have you come to harm out there in the dark."

"I'll be careful, I promise."

Mam as usual, was worrying unnecessarily. What could possibly happen to her if she wasn't stupid enough to fall into the pond or walk into a tree? It was Joey Leah was worried about. A lot of things could happen to a lost six-year-old on a night like this…none of them good.

Chapter Two

Twenty minutes after arriving at the Beachy farm, Daniel found himself trudging through a pasture in the rain with his cousins Caroline and Leslie, whom he would be staying with, and a young Amish woman, Leah Yoder. It was a strange turn of events. He'd expected to spend the evening giving his PowerPoint presentation, but this wasn't the first time that God had steered him in a new direction.

Daniel had learned to listen to his inner voice, and it had never failed him. No message had ever come stronger than the need to join in the hunt for little Joey Beachy and to enlist the Mennonite community in the search. His talk could be given another day. A child's life might be in danger, and Daniel couldn't stand by while others went out to find him.

Growing up, he'd often been rebellious. He

loved his parents and family, and he knew the importance of the missionary work that they did, but he'd never thought it was the life for him. When he'd left them in Morocco to go to college in the States, he'd insisted on a typical college experience. He hadn't even gone to the Mennonite Bible School that his parents and his older brother had attended. Instead, he'd gone to the University of Ohio to study nursing. He'd expected to work in a small community hospital in the Midwest when he graduated, but then, like now, God had other plans for him. In the end, he liked to think that his early rebellion against his parents' expectations had better prepared him for his life.

Daniel suddenly felt his foot slip in a water-filled hole and he threw his hands out to try to regain his balance. At the same moment, Leah grabbed his arm to steady him, keeping him from falling onto his bottom. "Thanks," he said as he righted himself, giving her a sheepish smile.

"Careful where you step," she cautioned. "You'll do Joey no good if you twist an ankle."

Leah's grip was strong. Being a farm girl, he supposed she must be used to lifting hay bales and chopping wood, but he still felt a little foolish. He should have been the one coming to *her* rescue.

Caroline giggled. "And watch out for the cow pies."

"Plenty of those out here too," Leah agreed, a hint of amusement in her voice.

"I'm good now." Daniel pulled away his hand, telling himself he shouldn't feel embarrassed. He'd have done the same for her, wouldn't he?

Daniel had been glad when Samuel Mast had picked Leah to accompany his group.

"She knows these woods and fields," Samuel had explained quietly to him. "We're glad for your help, but it's easy to get turned around out there if you don't know where you're going. You'll be all right with Leah. She's a sensible girl."

Watching Leah in the dark, Daniel thought that it was probably a good assessment. She was dressed for the downpour in boots and a rain slicker and she'd brought her own flashlight. She was keeping the strong beam steady to light their way.

In spite of the confusion at the Grange, Daniel had noticed red-haired Leah right away. Not only was she particularly attractive, but he'd been struck by how worldly she'd seemed for a young Amish woman. Her starched white *kapp* and modest blue dress and cape had looked exactly like those of her companions, but Leah Yoder stood out among them. She maintained a certain poise he didn't usually see in Amish women. It was immediately clear that she had a strong personality and was a take-charge type of person, all characteristics he admired.

Daniel remembered that when he was in Ohio recently, a cousin had talked at length about her Amish friend, Leah, from Delaware and the fun they'd had last summer at the county fair. He wondered if this could be the same Leah. It had to be. How many Amish Leahs could there be in Kent County, Delaware?

After all the search groups had been organized back in the barnyard, Samuel had suggested that each group choose a leader. Samuel had made a joke about Daniel not letting his girls get out of hand, and the other men had thought it funny.

Daniel ended up being the only man on an otherwise all-female team, but it didn't matter to him. He'd promised his Aunt Joyce, Caroline and Leslie's mother, that he'd look after them if they were allowed to help in the search. He had every intention of keeping his word, but once they'd left the barnyard, he suggested Leah take the leader's position in the group.

"You don't want to?" she'd asked. "I have to

warn you, you might get some teasing from the men if they hear about it."

"I'm not a country boy," he'd explained. "It would be foolish for me to tell you where we should look for Joey. You know the area. Besides, I'd get us all lost in the dark, and search parties would have to come find us."

Carolyn had chuckled. "He's right, Leah. Daniel's sense of direction isn't that great. He got lost at Hershey Park with his church group."

"I was only eight," Daniel had protested. "And the whole family has teased me about it ever since."

"Believe me," Caroline had said. "We're all safer if you lead the way, Leah."

"All right," Leah had agreed. "If you put it that way, but we may have to walk a long way and there will be fences to climb and briars to wade through."

"Lead on, Sacagawea," Daniel had said. "I promise not to wimp out."

And here they were now, in the dark, in the rain, mud sucking at Daniel's best leather shoes. His *only* pair of good shoes.

The pasture was huge. After they'd gone far enough that the house was only a small light in the distance, Caroline asked Leah if she knew how Joey had gotten lost in the first place.

Leah slowed her pace so that they could walk

closer together. "Barbara—that's Joey's sister—told me that their mother had sent Abraham and Minnie to find their Jersey cow."

"The Beachys must have a large family," Leslie remarked.

"Fairly large." Leah flashed the light across a hole to be sure they all saw it. "Joey has thirteen brothers and sisters."

"So what happened in this hunt for the cow?" Caroline asked.

"Abraham and Minnie went out looking for Matilda," Leah continued, keeping the flashlight beam steady ahead of them. "Watch out for that briar." She pointed. "The spines are sharp enough to go through your clothes."

"Who's Matilda?"

"Matilda is the cow. Matilda hadn't come in to be milked with the rest of the herd. Apparently she's due to drop her calf in a few weeks, and Lydia was concerned about her. Pregnant cows sometimes wander off and hide, and a rainy April night is no place for a newborn calf."

"Too cold, I suppose," Daniel offered. He didn't know a thing about cows, even less about cows having calves, but it seemed logical.

"True," Leah agreed. "But more than that, there's a pack of dogs in the neighborhood. Englishers like to drop their unwanted pets near our farms. I guess they think that we can take in every stray, but we can't. It's a real problem for farmers or anyone with livestock." She sighed deeply. "There are four or five dogs in this particular pack. I doubt they were abandoned together, but they found each other. Left to fend for themselves, eventually even pets turn feral. They kill squirrels and deer and rabbits to live, but they find their way into barnyards. Penned animals are easier prey. My Uncle Reuben lost a milk goat to them this winter. I'm sure Lydia was afraid that if Matilda dropped her calf, the dogs would smell the blood and come after them."

"Almost like wolves." Leslie looked around fearfully.

"Could these dogs be a danger to a child?" Caroline asked.

"I hope not, but you never know." Leah continued forward, lowering her head against the driving rain. "Anyway, Joey must have followed the bigger kids. When Abraham saw him, he was already angry with him because Joey had seen him accidentally spilling a bucket of milk this morning, and Joey had told their mother. Abraham got in trouble and, naturally, he blamed Joey, instead of his own carelessness."

"Like my little brothers," Caroline said. "They're always getting into it. I never realized that Amish mothers had the same trouble."

Leah chuckled. "We aren't that different," she

reminded. "We may offer our prayers in a different form and dress differently, but kids are kids."

"It's like that all over the world," Daniel put in. "But go on."

"Anyway," Leah continued. "It started to thunder, and Minnie got scared."

"How old is *she*?" Leslie wanted to know.

"Minnie's eight," Leah said. "She started crying to go back to the house. Annoyed because they hadn't found the cow and he still had chores to finish before dinner, Abraham told them both to go home. He told them he'd find Matilda himself."

"But if Joey was with his sister," Leslie said, "how did…"

"According to Minnie," Leah went on, "Joey had gone only a short distance with her when there was thunder again and he decided that he wanted Abraham. He left Minnie to run back to his brother, leaving Minnie to think he was with Abraham, and Abraham believing Minnie had taken him back to the house. Abraham eventually found the missing cow, and drove her back to the barn, but he never saw Joey."

"Was there a calf?" Caroline stopped to untangle herself from some tall weeds. The rain wasn't making it easier for any of them. Instead of letting up, it was coming down harder, and they were walking directly into it.

"No, Matilda was just being a cow." Leah slowed to wait for her. "They aren't as smart as horses or dogs, and they can be a little hard-headed. Anyway, no one missed Joey until his place was empty at the dinner table. By then he'd been missing for nearly two hours."

"Well, he's got to be out here somewhere." Leslie moved closer to Daniel. "There aren't any bulls in this pasture, are there?"

"The Beachys don't have a bull and the cows are all up at the barn." Leah made a small sound of distress. "I can't imagine being Joey's age and out here alone. Wherever he is, he must be terrified."

Across the field, Daniel could see flickering lights from other search parties' flashlights, but they were too far away to hear the volunteers. The only sounds besides their own footsteps and voices were the rain falling, the wind and the occasional rustle in the grass. Every so often, they stopped and Leah called the boy's name, but there was never an answer.

The house and barn were far behind them, and in the wet darkness, Daniel felt as though he was in a wilderness. He'd traveled all over the world, but he'd always lived in an urban environment. He was used to towns and teeming cities, airports and hospitals. He was at home in noisy bazaars and crowded neighborhoods where

Arabic and Spanish and a dozen other languages were spoken. He'd learned to feel at ease on busy trains, buses and subways, but here he felt completely out of his element. How could they possibly find one small child in all this darkness? Joey could be anywhere.

It was no wonder the Beachy family had called for help. Daniel had been told that women from the Amish church were organizing a prayer vigil, and he knew that Dinah Rhinehart had asked the Mennonite women if they would do the same. Samuel Mast said that someone had notified the Delaware State Police. And in the farmyard, Daniel had heard talk of sending for search dogs.

"There are a lot of rumors flying around," Leah said when they stopped to catch their breath. "One of the Beachy girls said that Joey had told her that a man in a blue pickup offered him candy at their mailbox a few days ago."

Daniel and his cousins moved closer so that they could hear what she was saying.

"And Noodle Troyer told my brother-in-law, Charley, that Elmer, Joey's brother, found Joey's hat and one shoe in the mud beside a pond. But I don't put much stock in that story, since it's Noodle." She cocked her head to one side. "He's known for telling tall tales and making much out of nothing."

Rain was running down the back of Daniel's

jean jacket, and his trousers were soaked. He wished he'd checked the weather report before heading north to Delaware from where he'd been speaking in Virginia—he could have used his raincoat right now. Leah was the only one who seemed to be properly dressed for a night like this. She had a hooded rain slicker that reached past her knees to her black rubber boots. Wide sleeves protected her arms and covered half her hands. Her flashlight was an expensive Maglite. His flashlight was a cheap one from the dollar store, and it wasn't as bright. It needed new batteries; he remembered that now. But he didn't always think ahead, a fault his father was quick to point out.

"Did you have time to stop home for your flashlight?" Daniel asked, giving his a tap.

"We always keep it in the buggy." Leah offered a quick smile. "Just to be safe. And it looked like rain, so I threw boots and the raincoat in the back before we headed to the Grange to hear the speaker. My mother always told us girls to be prepared for anything whenever we left home."

"She sounds wise, your mother," Daniel said.

"*Ya,* Mam is smart. She's the schoolteacher here in Seven Poplars. But she's got a lot of common sense, too."

"What else do you carry in case of emergencies?" Daniel asked. He was teasing her a little, but he was also curious. There were all sorts of things about Leah Yoder he wanted to know.

"I have flares in the buggy, too," she answered, "but I didn't see any need to bring those."

"You don't have a cell phone, do you?"

"Nah." Leah shook her head, sending droplets of water flying. "Our church doesn't permit them."

"Don't you have a phone, Daniel?" Caroline asked. "I keep telling Mom that I need one just as much as Leslie does."

"I do have a cell," Daniel admitted, "but it's back in my truck. I forgot to charge it, so it wouldn't be much use to us. But if Leslie brought hers…"

"I've got it," Leslie assured him, patting the pocket of her coat. "And it's charged."

"We don't have electricity so a cell phone wouldn't do me much good," Leah explained. "There's a regular phone at the chair shop across the road from our house. We can use it to call the doctor or make important calls, but we aren't allowed to have personal phones."

Daniel liked Leah's voice. It was clear and sweet, yet she had no trouble making herself heard above the rain. Leah had a slight accent, not German, but almost Southern. Her grammar and vocabulary were very good. Hearing her, no one would guess that she'd never completed high school. The Delaware Amish, he knew, sent their children to private church schools that ended with eighth-grade graduation.

"There's a fence just ahead," Leah said. "I thought maybe we should search the woods, but I see lights there so I think some of the other groups are looking there. If we cross the fence line, we'll be on the Crawford sheep farm. The Crawfords are living in Dover while their house is being remodeled, and there's a long lane from the road to the buildings."

Using his little flashlight, Daniel located a fence post and three strands of barbed wire. "How do we climb over that?" he asked.

"We don't." Leah plucked at the top row. "But the wire isn't tight. If one of us holds up that bottom strand, the others can crawl under."

Daniel nodded, resigned to whatever it took to find the boy. He was already wet and cold, so what was a little mud? "I'll hold the wire until you get through, and then one of you can hold it for me."

The plan worked, but the ground was just as wet and uncomfortable as he thought it would be. He supposed that a six-year-old would have had an easier time getting under, if he'd come this way. But why would a child venture farther away from home rather than closer? He felt a sense of dread. What if the rumor about Joey's hat and shoe discovered by the pond was true? Or, God forbid, the story about a stranger offering the boy a treat? Tonight could end in more than discomfort. It could be a real tragedy for the Beachy family and the whole community.

"Please, God," he murmured under his breath as he wiggled the last few inches until he was clear of the barbed wire. "Be with this child. Hold him safe in the palm of your hand until we can get to him."

"Ouch!" Caroline cried.

Daniel got to his feet. "What's wrong? Did you hurt yourself?" He shone his flashlight on Caroline. She was holding her left hand out, and even through the rain, he could see that blood was oozing from a deep gash across her palm.

"Let me see," he said. On closer inspection, he saw that the cut was ragged and about two inches long.

"Does it hurt?" Leslie asked.

"It stings."

"That barbed wire is rusty." Leah came to stand with them. "I hope you're up-to-date on your tetanus shot."

"She was vaccinated when she was little," Leslie said. "Isn't that good enough?"

"I don't think so," Leah said. "Irwin—he's sort

of my foster brother—stepped on a nail a couple of weeks ago and our doctor said he had to have a booster. She'll probably need to have one, too, but it's not an emergency. It can wait until tomorrow as long as she doesn't need stitches."

"I don't think it needs stitches." Daniel handed his cousin a handkerchief. "But Leah's right. You should check with your doctor to see when you were last vaccinated. I've actually seen cases of tetanus. It's not something to mess around with."

Caroline wrapped his handkerchief around her hand, but the cloth turned from white to pink. "I feel like such an idiot. I thought I had hold of the wire, but it slipped through my hand."

"I think you'd better go back to the house." Leslie rested her hand on Caroline's back. "Mom will want to have a look at this."

"But I wanted to help." Caroline's voice quivered. "And now, I've caused all of you a problem."

"Why don't the three of you go back?" Leah suggested. "I want to check some sheds on this farm, but I'll be fine. I know the way."

Daniel reached out and pressed his hand over Caroline's. "More pressure should stop the bleeding. Do you think you'll be all right to walk back with Leslie?"

"Sure," she answered. "It's a cut hand, not a broken leg."

"Leslie?" he asked. "You okay walking her back?"

"Sure. I'll go with her. I hate to leave you guys, but I agree she shouldn't go alone. What if she faints or something?"

Caroline made a sound of disbelief. "Have you ever known me to faint in my life? Stop making such a fuss. I'll be fine. You stay and hunt for Joey with Daniel and Leah. I can go back myself."

"I don't think that's a good idea." Daniel adjusted his ball cap to try to keep some of the rain out of his eyes. "The two of you should go back together. No one should be out here alone. I'll go with Leah." He looked at Leah as it occurred to him what he was saying. Three girls and a guy was one thing. A guy and girl, in some cultures, was something entirely different. "Will you be in trouble if the two of us go on together alone? We're not breaking any Amish rules, are we?"

"Nah," Leah assured him. "It isn't encouraged, a boy and girl alone together, but it's not forbidden. We're looking for a lost child. It's not like we're dating or anything."

Caroline giggled.

Leah glanced at Caroline, then back at Daniel. "This kind of situation allows for exceptions to the rules. Besides, I haven't officially joined the Amish church, so I'm sort of *rumspringa*. This is my running around time. The rules aren't so strict for me."

"So you don't mind if I come with you?"

Leah shook her head. "I would be glad of your help. But we have to get going." She looked out over the dark field ahead. "I have a bad feeling about this," she said softly. "A really bad feeling."

Chapter Three

Daniel watched as Caroline and Leslie's flash-light beam grew smaller as they recrossed the big pasture beyond the barbed-wire fence. "I guess it's just the two of us," he said to Leah, raising his voice so that she could hear him above the sound of the rain and the booming thunder.

"Just the two of us," she repeated. "Come on. This way. It doesn't look as though this is going to let up."

Not only wasn't the downpour easing, it was getting worse. He glanced up as lightning zig-zagged through the sky. It struck so close that he smelled the burnt grass when a bolt hit the ground. "Maybe we should think about looking for shelter," Daniel suggested, not so much worried for himself as for Leah. "Just until the worst of this passes."

"There's a shed in the pasture beyond these

woods where the farmer stores hay," Leah shouted. "We can duck in there." She began to walk faster, and he lengthened his stride to keep up with her.

Water was running down the inside of Daniel's jacket, and his pants were soaked and muddy to his knees. Leah was wearing a skirt, so he knew she had to be colder than he was, even wearing her rain slicker. He couldn't imagine any of his sisters out here in the dark and pouring rain with a strange man. The two still at home were both younger than he supposed Leah must be, but he doubted they would ever have the self-confidence that she seemed to have. Most girls, especially girls born with such outer beauty as Leah possessed, rarely showed the same strength of character.

A gust of wind shook the trees overhead and nearly knocked them off their feet. Daniel took Leah's arm to steady her, and she made no protest. *A night like this and a child lost in it? What must the boy's family be going through?*

Once, when his family was sightseeing in Barcelona, his younger brother, Matthew, had gotten separated from the rest of them during a festival. The streets were crowded, and eight-year-old Matthew spoke only a little Spanish. They'd notified the police and looked for Matthew for hours without finding a trace of him.

Daniel remembered how pale his mother's face had been, and yet, she'd remained calm. "Have faith, but don't stop hunting for him," she'd said. "God expects us to do our fair share."

Their prayers had been answered. When his mother had returned to the bed-and-breakfast where they'd been staying, Matthew was sitting on the steps waiting. Earlier that morning, he had picked up a brochure in the hotel because it had red balloons on it. He'd stuck the folder in his coat pocket, and when he got lost, he'd asked a teenage girl for help. She'd studied English in school and was able to understand why Matthew was crying. Somehow, the girl had seen the brochure, read the address, and given his little brother a ride back to the B&B on the back of her bike.

"Lucky," the policeman had said, when Daniel's parents had reported Matthew as safe.

"Not lucky, but blessed," Mother had insisted.

Daniel hoped that Joey Beachy would be just as blessed. He was even younger than Matthew had been, and the family still talked about the incident. Daniel missed his family, but he missed his little brother most of all. This would have been Matthew's senior year in high school, but he'd moved to Canada with their mother, father and the three girls. Daniel hoped he'd have time to visit with them before he left for his new assignment.

Lightning flashed, closer this time, and Daniel felt a little better when they left the trees. The batteries in his flashlight were growing weaker, however, and the beam was a pale yellow light. "I think it's going out," he said to Leah, tapping the flashlight against his leg.

"Don't worry," she said. "Mine's good."

As if on cue, his flashlight went out. He smacked it against his leg, but it wouldn't come back on.

"It's okay. We're almost there." She pointed with her flashlight, and Daniel made out a dark outline of a wooden gate in the tall grass.

"I see it," he shouted, shoving his useless flashlight into his jacket pocket. He didn't have much hope that little Joey would be this far from the house, but once the worst of the storm passed, maybe they could double-back to continue their search.

They dashed the last few yards to the shelter. Leah shone her flashlight on the wooden gate and Daniel tugged it open. The first thing that he saw when he stepped into the shed was the pale frightened face of a small boy looking up at him.

"Joey!" Leah cried.

Little Joey Beachy sat on the ground with his

arms around a shaggy brown-and-white goat. His eyes were red and swollen from crying; streaks trailed down his dirty cheeks. When he saw Leah, a cascade of fresh tears began to flow.

"Joey," Leah crooned, setting her flashlight on a bale of hay. She dropped to her knees and gathered the child into her arms. "What are you doing here?" she murmured. "Your mam is so worried. Everyone's been hunting for you."

Joey began to sob. Daniel couldn't understand what he was saying because the boy was speaking Pennsylvania Dutch. Leah switched to that language as well, leaving Daniel at a loss. He glanced around the low shed. It was too dark to see much, but the roof was sound, and it was a relief to be out of the downpour.

The goat got up and began bleating pitifully. Daniel didn't know much about goats, but this one sounded as if it was in distress. Daniel's wet coat clung to him. It was so soaked through that it gave little protection against the cold, so he took it off and draped it over a bale of hay. Then another sound, a feeble high-pitched squeak, caught his attention.

Leah must have heard the noise as well, because she turned her flashlight toward the source. Nestled in the hay was a baby goat. Daniel hadn't noticed it before because it was black and nearly hidden in the shadows. The larger goat nosed at the little one, looked back at her midsection and began to bleat again.

Daniel didn't need translation. As an RN, he'd had a rotation in maternity at Rutherford General Hospital. He hadn't seen any pregnant goats there, but he'd helped deliver a lot of babies. And now that he looked at the brown-and-white goat closely, he could see that her belly was still swollen. She'd just given birth to the little black kid but was obviously carrying a second one.

Leah hugged Joey and stood him on his feet, wiping under his eyes with her thumbs. "He said that he got separated from his brother and sister and a wolf chased him."

"A wolf?"

She shrugged, but her eyes twinkled. "He said he ran to the shelter to get away from the wolf and found the goat here."

Joey nodded and started talking again in Pennsylvania Dutch.

"English," Leah reminded him.

"The baby. I didn't want the wolf to get it," the boy said. "Then it was night and…and…" A rattle of Dutch followed.

"He was afraid of the storm," Leah finished. "And he couldn't leave the goats. The doe is having trouble."

Daniel nodded. "I think there's a second kid."

"Probably," she agreed.

Daniel picked up her flashlight and shone the beam around the shed, seeing that the roof slanted toward the back. Bales of sweet-smelling hay were stacked against the far wall, making the shelter feel snug and almost warm.

"So he stayed here all this time with the goats?" Daniel asked.

"He was afraid the wolves would kill them. It was probably the wild dogs I was telling you about." She rubbed the boy's arm, said something in Pennsylvania Dutch again, then continued speaking to Daniel in English. "A goat can usually drive off a single dog, but not a pack. Joey was smart to stay here where it was safe."

The mother goat began to paw the floor and bleat. Leah walked over to the goat and ran her hands over its belly. "I think the twin kid might be stuck," she said. "The first one is already dry. This one should have been born by now." She bit down on her lower lip. "I wish my sister, Miriam, was here. She'd know what to do." She looked up at Daniel. "She's really good with animals."

"Can you hold her?" Daniel asked, putting the flashlight back on the bale of hay. He dug into the deep pockets of his jacket and pulled out a pair of latex gloves he always carried. "If you can hold her still, I can examine her."

Joey said something in Pennsylvania Dutch.

"He wants to know if you know about goats."

"Not so much about goats," Daniel admitted. "But I'm a nurse. I know about babies. Goats can't be much different, can they?" He couldn't see Leah's face in the shadows, but he sensed that she was looking at him in a different way.

"You're a nurse?" she asked softly. "I thought nurses were women."

"Not all nurses." This shed wasn't the ideal spot for a delivery. He was used to the sterile conditions of a hospital. He put his hands on the goat and she squealed and tried to get away.

"Wait," Leah grabbed her flashlight off the bale of hay and handed it to the boy. "Hold it steady, Joey. I'll hold the doe." She slipped her arms around the goat's neck and pushed against its front legs with her knee. To Daniel's surprise, the doe's legs folded under her and she lay down on the hay-strewn floor.

With Leah holding the animal still, it was much easier for him to run his hands along its abdomen. "I think I see the problem," he said. "One of the kid's legs is twisted back, keeping it from being born."

"Is there anything you can do to help?" Leah asked softly.

Daniel liked the way she remained calm. He could imagine what the reaction of most girls would be, but she was different, more mature...

sensible. He found he liked Leah Yoder more and more as the night wore on.

"If you can keep her still, I think I can wiggle that leg free and…yes, there it comes!"

The goat leaped to her feet and a moment later, another kid slipped out into the straw on the floor. The baby was still encased in the birth sac, a clear bubble; it wasn't moving. Daniel pulled the membrane away from the nose and mouth, and began to rub the tiny body.

"Is it dead?" Joey asked, holding on to Leah's raincoat.

The mother goat nosed the kid.

Daniel kept massaging the baby. Lifting the head, he scooped out the mouth and wiped the nose clean. "He's tired, poor little thing," Daniel explained softly. He picked up a handful of hay and began to rub the damp hide briskly. "Sometimes, all it takes is—"

The baby choked, coughed and let out a wail. The doe pushed past Daniel and began to lick her second newborn. In minutes, the tiny newborn was on its feet and jostling the older twin for a turn at the mother's teats.

"You saved them," Leah said, getting to her feet. "I didn't think…"

"Ya," Joey agreed, returning the flashlight to Leah. "You saved them." He knelt beside the little goats and petted first one and then the other.

"The mother might have been able to deliver it." Daniel didn't want to appear to take too much credit for doing what he'd been trained to do. But secretly, he was thrilled. He'd felt that way whenever he'd seen a new life come into the world. It never failed to strengthen his faith in God. How could anyone watch a newborn take a deep breath, look around and not see God's wonderful plan? He allowed himself a deep sigh of satisfaction and pulled off the gloves.

"I think the brunt of the storm has passed." Leah listened for a moment. "I think it's safe to go out again. We should get Joey home to his mother."

"But the goats," the boy protested. "The bad wolf might come and—"

"We'll lock the gate," Leah assured him. "The goats will be fine until the farmer comes tomorrow." She took Joey's hand. "Daniel?"

"It's still pretty nasty out there," he said, glancing into the dark as he grabbed his wet jacket. The rain was still coming down, though not as hard as before. "Maybe you and Joey should stay here while I go for—"

Leah laughed, her flashlight beam steady on the gate. "And do you remember the way back to the Beachy farm? Or will we have to send a search party out for you?"

He chuckled and looked down at his wet shoes. "You're probably right."

"I am. Now come on…we'll go together. All three of us."

"I guess we do make a pretty good team," Daniel dared. He liked the sound of her laughter. She was teasing him, but not in a mocking way. She was teasing as a friend might tease another friend. It gave him a good feeling; he'd made a good friend in Seven Poplars. He had a big family, but in their travels it hadn't always been easy to make friends and keep them. Leah was a special young woman, and he hoped he'd see her again after tonight.

The walk back to Joey's house didn't seem as far as it had on the way out. Another search party met up with them in the pasture. Joey's uncle was with them, and he'd whooped for joy and picked the boy up and carried him back to the house on his shoulders.

At the Beachy house, the adults and most of the children were still awake. Men stood on the porch and outside the back door drinking cups of steaming black coffee, and someone thrust a cup into Daniel's hand. Joey was hugged and fussed over and trundled off into the house by his mother and a gaggle of women. Leah was caught up in the crowd and vanished along with the boy.

"Good work for a city boy," Samuel Mast said as he slapped Daniel on the back. He was grinning. Everyone was.

"Leah Yoder deserves the credit," Daniel insisted. "She was the one who thought to go where the hay was stored. The weather had gotten so bad, I thought we should turn back."

"But if the boy wasn't hurt, why didn't he run home before it got dark?" A bearded Amish man stuck his hand out and Daniel shook it. "Roman Byler," he said. "I own the chair shop down the road."

Daniel began to explain about the dog that Joey thought was a wolf that had chased him and the pregnant goat. Before he knew it, Joey's mother was ushering Daniel into the house and waving him to a place at the table. Other men were already there, eating sandwiches and vegetable soup.

"To warm your insides," Joey's father said.

Daniel hadn't thought he was hungry, but after the first bite, he remembered that he hadn't eaten anything since he'd stopped for lunch on the interstate at about one o'clock. After the mishap at the rest stop, when he'd left his coat, he'd ended up running late and hadn't had time to stop and eat before he reached Seven Poplars. The ham sandwich was good, and the soup delicious. He hadn't had a better meal since he'd last sat at his mother's table.

The large kitchen was overflowing with men and women, most talking to each other in Pennsylvania Dutch, laughing and joking. Daniel was surprised by how at home he felt here among these people, even though he didn't speak their language. But the one person he kept looking for he didn't see. He'd wanted to tell Leah how much he appreciated her help and what a great job she'd done. Soon the sun would be coming up, and he was tired. He hated to leave without saying goodbye to Leah.

Finally, when the men began to take their leave, Daniel stood, thanked his host and hostess and made his way out to where he'd left his pickup truck. Buggies were rolling out of the farmyard, and men, hands in pockets, walked off into the soft darkness.

He was disappointed that he hadn't seen Leah, but he knew he should go. Even though his aunt knew where he was, she'd be worried about him. He put his hand on the driver's door handle and was about to get into his truck when Leah appeared from around the back of the pickup.

"A goodnight to you, Daniel Steiner," she said.

He looked up at her. "Excuse me?"

"I said goodnight to you, Daniel Steiner," she repeated.

"I'm not Daniel Steiner."

"You're not?" Leah sounded confused. "But I thought you were Caroline's cousin and—"

"Oh," he said, understanding the mixup. "Caroline is my cousin. She's a Steiner, but her mother is my aunt. I'm a Brown, Daniel Brown."

"Daniel Brown." Her pretty blue eyes widened. "*The* Daniel Brown…the speaker we were supposed to hear tonight?"

"That's me." Feeling awkward, he slipped his hands into his pockets. He really liked Leah, so much so that he didn't want to say goodbye. "We're going to reschedule for another night this coming week. I hope you…you and your friends can come back."

"*You're* the Daniel Brown—the hero who saved that boy from the mob?"

"Hardly a hero," Daniel protested.

"I didn't know…" She hesitated. "Now I feel foolish. I spent the whole night with you and I never asked you about your travels. I never…" She stopped and started again. "I really feel foolish."

"Don't. It was a natural mistake." He struggled to find the right thing to say. He didn't want her to walk away feeling embarrassed. "I'll be looking for you—at the presentation. I hope you aren't disappointed."

"Ne," Leah said. "You couldn't disappoint anyone, Daniel Brown. Least of all me."

"I'll see you there, then?"

"Leah?" A woman called from the porch. "Are you ready?"

"Ya," she answered. "Coming." She smiled at him. "I'm glad you were with me tonight."

"Me, too."

"What you said before," she murmured shyly. "I agree. We made a good team."

"We did," he concurred. And then she turned and hurried off, leaving him standing there staring after her and wishing she wasn't going.

Chapter Four

The following morning, as golden rays of April sunlight spilled through the bedroom window, Leah sighed and snuggled deeper beneath the crisp blue and white Bear's Paw quilt that had been her Christmas gift from her eldest sister, Johanna. Below Leah's window, from a perch on the top rail of the garden fence, a wayward rooster crowed. *Just a few more minutes,* Leah thought, burrowing under her pillow. *All I want is a few more...*

A high-pitched giggle pierced her groggy haze. "You a-wake, Leah? Mam made pancakes!"

Leah caught the scent of fresh coffee, felt the mattress bounce and groaned. It had been nearly daylight when she'd finally gotten to bed, and she couldn't have had more than three hours' sleep.

"An' bacon!" proclaimed the cheerful voice.

Leah opened one eye and smiled into the round, red-cheeked face hovering only inches from her own. "Morning, Susanna-banana," she mumbled.

Her sister giggled again. "I'm not a banana. Get up, silly. I'm hungry." She pushed a mug of coffee under Leah's nose. "Brought you coffee." It came out sounding more like *toffee*, but Leah had no trouble understanding Susanna's sometimes childish speech.

"You're always hungry," Leah replied, but it was impossible to remain out of sorts with Susanna, even too early on a visiting Sunday when there was no church and they could sleep in. Her sister was such a sweet-natured soul that simply being near her made Leah smile. "Thanks for the coffee. Tell Mam I'll be downstairs in two shakes of a lamb's tail."

"'Kay." Susanna's mouth widened in a grin as she scooted off the bed, carefully sliding the brimming cup to the end of the nightstand. Then she trotted out of the bedroom and down the hall toward the stairs.

Leah stretched and rubbed her eyes before reaching for the coffee. As always, Susanna had sweetened it to her own taste and drowned it in heavy cream, but it was hot and bracing and washed some of the sleep out of Leah's brain. Yawning, she padded barefoot to the window and threw up the sash. The sun was already high, and the sky was a robin's-egg blue without a hint of clouds. Spread out before her were Mam's kitchen garden, rich farm fields and fruit trees in the first blossom of spring.

"Thank you, God," she murmured as she breathed in the sweet smell of newly turned soil and fresh-cut grass. "Thank you for keeping Joey safe through the stormy night and letting us find him." Closing her eyes, she offered a simple and silent prayer, asking His blessing on her family and community and for guidance through the coming day.

Almost instantly, a sense of contentment and pure joy washed over her. How was it possible that last night, an evening that had started so fearful, had turned out to be so wonderful?

Not only had Joey been returned to his family without harm, but she'd met a dynamic stranger and helped him deliver a new life into the world. Goose bumps rose on Leah's bare arms as she exhaled softly. Nothing like that ever happened in Seven Poplars, but it *had* happened last night, and she'd been part of it. She couldn't wait to tell her sisters about her adventure, especially Johanna. Of all of them, Johanna shared her sometimes rebellious spirit and would understand best how she felt.

Leah had loved coming home after almost

a year in Ohio taking care of *Grossmama,* but things here had quickly fallen back into the ordinary. Not exactly boring… There were always chores to do and new challenges to face, especially now that Anna had married Samuel in a whirlwind romance, leaving only Susanna, Rebecca, Irwin and her at home to help Mam. But after the hustle and bustle of *Grossmama's* more liberal Amish community, her new Mennonite friends, and the relative independence she and Rebecca had experienced in Ohio, it wasn't easy settling in under Mam's authority again. And she did have to admit to herself that sometimes Seven Poplar's conservative customs seemed a little old-fashioned.

So many changes, Leah thought wistfully. When she and Rebecca had left for Ohio last year, the house had been bursting with unmarried sisters, and when they'd returned, three had found husbands, and Mam had hired and then practically adopted Irwin, a thirteen-year-old orphaned boy who had lived with Joey Beachy's family. It all took a little getting used to.

Not that her beloved sisters were far away; Miriam and Ruth were just across the field in the little farmhouse with their new husbands, and Anna and Samuel's farm was next door. But they had their own families and households, and it wasn't the same as waking up every morning to a gaggle of giggling girls or having so many to share secrets and gossip with after the lights had been blown out at night. Plus, Grandmother Yoder, no longer able to live alone, and her sister, Aunt Jezebel, were now part of Mam's household.

Grossmama was going to live with Anna and Samuel this summer. Anna had wanted her to move in sooner, but Mam had been firm. She'd insisted that Anna needed a few months to adjust to being a wife and mother to Samuel's five children before taking on *Grossmama*, no matter how well the two of them got on together. That would leave Aunt Jezebel here, but compared to her sister, Aunt Jezzy was a dream.

"What's taking you so long?" Rebecca called from the doorway. "You aren't even dressed." She came in and plopped onto the unmade bed. "*Grossmama* won't be happy if her pancakes are cold."

Leah rolled her eyes and forced back a snappy response. "Sorry. I didn't expect anyone to wait breakfast on me this morning." She went to the corner where her clothing hung and took down a fresh shift and a lavender-colored dress.

"Mam said not to wear that," Rebecca said. "Wear your good blue one. Aunt Martha thinks that the lavender is too short, and she's bound to come visiting today. She'll want to hear all about that Mennonite preacher you were running around with in the dark last night."

Leah wrinkled her nose. "Since when does Mam take Aunt Martha's advice on what we should wear?"

Rebecca shrugged. "I'm just telling you what Mam said. I think Mam thinks it's too short, too."

Leah's mouth puckered as she hung the lavender dress with its neat tailoring back on the hook and took down the dark blue one her mother had given her for her birthday. Leah liked the blue. It went well with her eyes and her dark auburn hair, but she was particularly fond of the lavender dress she and her Mennonite friend, Sophie Steiner, had cut and stitched. Sophie's mother had a new electric-powered Singer that practically sewed a garment for you. Maybe the lavender was a little shorter than the blue dress, but it covered her knees and the neckline and sleeves were modest enough to satisfy even the bishop.

"And your good *kapp*," Rebecca added. "No scarf today."

Leah sighed. She and Rebecca had spent so much time together in the last year that they should have been as close as Ruth and Miriam, but somehow, this sister always brought out the worst in her. She loved Rebecca dearly, but they were just too different to have the relationship she had with Johanna or dear Anna. Leah loved to be doing something with her hands: picking blueberries, making jam or selling vegetables to the English tourists at Spence's Auction. By contrast, Rebecca was happiest at home, drinking tea with Mam or Aunt Jezebel, reading a prayer book or writing a letter for publication in the *Budget*.

Rebecca never questioned the rules. She'd always been the good girl of the family, the serious one. She'd been baptized at age sixteen, before she'd even ventured into the outside world. It never occurred to Rebecca to be cross with Aunt Martha for her criticizing or bossy ways. In Leah's mind, Rebecca was simply too meek for her own good. And worse, Rebecca couldn't understand why Leah sometimes longed to kick out of the traces, and why, at almost twenty-one, she had yet to make the lifelong commitment to join the Amish Church.

Leah gathered her brush, *kapp* and her clean underclothes and started for the bathroom. "I'll be quick," she promised her sister. "Tell Mam, five minutes."

"What was he like?" Rebecca asked.

"Who?"

Rebecca raised an eyebrow. "You know who. The Mennonite preacher. Was he as fast as they say?"

Annoyed, Leah stopped short and glanced

back over her shoulder. "As fast as *who* says? Who around here knows him well enough to say something like that? That he's fast?"

Her sister smiled. "It's what they say about all Mennonite boys, isn't it? People say that they're wild, that they try to take liberties with Amish girls."

"That's nonsense. And Daniel isn't a boy. He must be twenty-five, maybe older."

Rebecca snickered. "And it's just *Daniel* now, is it? But then you probably got to know him well out there in the woods. He didn't try to steal a kiss, did he?"

"No. He didn't. And Daniel Brown's not a preacher. He's a nurse, a good one."

"And you know that how?"

"Because he helped a baby goat to be born when we were out looking for Joey. It was stuck, a leg tangled. The nanny would have died and the kid with her if Daniel hadn't known what to do."

"So he's not a preacher. But he is a missionary. He must have been lots of places, known lots of English girls. Fancy foreign girls, too."

"I suppose he has, but he was nice. *Is* nice. And when he gives his program, I'm going to be there to hear it."

"If Mam lets you go again."

Leah's brow creased as she tried to hide the

annoyance she felt at Rebecca's words. *"Ne, sister,"* she answered softly. "That's not what I said. I said I'm going to hear Daniel's talk and see the pictures of Spain and Morocco. I'll be twenty-one in a few weeks, and I'm an adult. I think I can decide for myself if I'm going to hear a missionary speak about his experiences in spreading God's word, *without* asking for my mother's permission."

Rebecca slid off the bed, moisture gleaming in her dark eyes. "I've made you angry."

Leah shook her head. "Not angry."

"Ya." A single tear blossomed on Rebecca's cheek. "I never say the right thing to you, Leah. I try, but it always comes out wrong. I worry about you."

Leah opened her arms and Rebecca came into them. Leah enveloped her in a hug. "Worry about me? Why? Because I hunted for a lost child last night—"

"Ne." Her sister switched from English to Pennsylvania Dutch. "You have a good heart. It was wrong of me to tease you about the Mennonite boy. I only did it because I'm frightened that we might lose you."

"Lose me?" Leah pulled away to look down into her sister's face. Rebecca was a small girl, like Miriam, not tall like Mam's side of the family. "How could you lose me?"

Rebecca clasped her hand and squeezed it hard. "You move too easily in the outside world. Since we were children, you always have. The English don't make you uncomfortable, as they do me."

"But why should that frighten you?"

"We're *Plain* folk—we're a people apart. Do you forget the martyrs who died that we might worship according to our beliefs?"

Leah leaned close and brushed a kiss on her sister's temple. "How could I forget? Being who I am—who we are—is bred into me, blood and bone. Surely, listening to a Mennonite tell about his mission work doesn't change that."

"It's not just that." Another tear followed the first. "It was the Mennonite friends you made out in Ohio. You went to their charity auctions, and you went to the fair with Jeanine and Sophie. And at least once, you helped out at their bake sale for their church."

"I did, but that was to raise money for a mission in the Ukraine. They wanted to send books and school supplies to orphans in a remote town. I wasn't attending worship services. And going to a fair to look at animals and eat cotton candy doesn't mean that I've forsaken my own faith," Leah protested. "I haven't."

Rebecca's chin quivered. "Everyone thought that you'd start classes for baptism this spring, but you didn't. Even Ruth is concerned about you. She and Aunt Jezzy were talking about it last week after church."

"And Mam? What does she say?"

Her sister sighed. "You know Mam. She just smiles and says, 'All in God's time.' But it's past time, Leah. You're the prettiest girl in Kent County, but you've never had a steady boyfriend, and you don't even let any boys drive you home from frolics and singings."

Leah wrinkled her nose again as she thought of Menno Swartzentruber, who'd tried to get her to ride home in his buggy last Sunday. "Maybe I haven't met the right boy. The ones around here seem too young and flighty." Menno was a hard worker, but his idea of a good joke was piling straw bales across the road to stop traffic in the dark or filling a paper bag with cow manure and leaving it on an Englisher's porch. No, she couldn't see herself dating Menno.

"And what about Jake King from the fourth district church? He's what? Twenty-eight or twenty-nine? He likes you, and you can't think Jake's too young."

"I like Jake—he's a good man. But his wife's only been dead six months. I wouldn't feel right walking out with Jake so soon after his loss."

"You see how you are." Rebecca stepped away and straightened her *kapp*, which had come loose when they'd hugged. "You always have a good excuse. But wearing that Ohio-style dress doesn't help. You know how people are—how they will talk. They start to wonder if you are drifting away from us."

"It sounds as though you've been talking to Aunt Martha," Leah said. "Or Dorcas."

"Aunt Martha has a sharp tongue," Rebecca admitted. "But she means well. She knows Dat would have been worried about you."

"You miss him a lot, don't you?" Leah murmured. Their father had been dead almost three years, but the hurt hadn't faded. Rebecca had taken the loss especially hard.

"I do."

"Me, too," she admitted softly.

"Leah! Leah!"

Both Leah and Rebecca turned toward the stairs as the clatter of footsteps echoed down the hallway.

"Leah! There's a man!" Susanna's eyes were wide, her cheeks red with excitement. "In a truck! In the kitchen!"

"A truck in Mam's kitchen?" Leah teased.

"Ne!" Susanna was breathless from running up the steps. "An Englisher man. He wants…" She inhaled deeply. "He wants you!"

Chapter Five

As Leah hurried down the front staircase, she suspected that she knew just which Englisher was waiting in the kitchen for her. It could only be Daniel Brown, and the thought that he'd come to her home so soon after leaving her at the Beachy farm a few hours ago made her pulse race.

What she wasn't expecting was to see Daniel seated at the head of the table in her father's chair, the one always ready to welcome guests. When she stepped through the doorway and Daniel saw her, he immediately rose to his feet. "Leah." His intense green-eyed gaze locked with hers, and her heart skipped a beat. "Good morning," he said with a smile.

Suddenly too shy to speak, she nodded and patted her *kapp*. She'd dressed so quickly that she wasn't entirely sure she was put together.

"I hope…" Daniel began.

"Yes?"

"You got some sleep?"

Leah nodded again. "Yes, I did." She didn't miss her grandmother's frown of disapproval. *Grossmama* didn't have to say a word. Her expression left no doubt as to what she was thinking. *Disgraceful*! A Mennonite boy come to seek out one of her unmarried granddaughters—more evidence of Leah's unorthodox behavior.

"The sun is shining," Daniel said, all in a rush. "After last night…I mean…after the rain."

"It is," Leah stammered. Behind her, she heard Rebecca stifle a giggle. "A beautiful morning," she added, feeling foolish. What was wrong with her that she was suddenly tongue-tied, unable to think of anything sensible to say? Daniel must think her a wooden head. "It happens a lot," she finished. "A beautiful sunny day after a storm."

"Yes, it seems that way," he answered.

"Sit, please," Leah said. Her stomach felt as though she'd swallowed a live moth. She clasped her hands together, and then smoothed her apron. When she'd first stepped out of the hall and seen Daniel at the table with her family, the kitchen had felt warm and welcoming, but *Grossmama*'s tight-lipped stare was quickly frosting the air.

Leah sucked in her breath, realizing that Daniel had displeased her grandmother even more by standing when Leah came into the room. It wasn't *Plain* behavior and went against the beliefs of the Old Order Amish.

Standing up when a woman joined them was what Leah had seen Englishers do in restaurants or on TV. Of course, television and movies were frowned upon by the church elders, but Leah was fascinated by glimpses of the outer world. Her Mennonite girlfriends had a television set in their family room, and Leah had watched Disney movies and some family shows with them on Saturday evenings when she was in Ohio. But she wasn't in Ohio now—she was in Kent County, Delaware, and Daniel's action had reminded everyone that he was an outsider.

"I didn't mean to intrude on your breakfast," Daniel said. "I wanted to invite you all to come back and…" He paused for breath and her mother finished the explanation.

"Daniel's program at the Grange will be this evening," Hannah said. "He wanted to make sure that we knew about it."

"He missed his breakfast this morning so he wouldn't be late for church," Aunt Jezzy put in. *Grossmama* glared at her, but Aunt Jezzy went on in her timid voice to say, "Hannah asked him to eat with us."

"I really didn't need to eat—" Daniel began.

Thirteen-year-old Irwin cut him off. "Don't

just stand there, Leah. Come to the table before the pancakes get cold."

Susanna and Rebecca took their places, but Leah glanced at her mother. The only seat left was her usual one, and that was next to Daniel. Leah could feel those moth wings fluttering in the pit of her stomach. If she sat beside Daniel, *Grossmama* would assume she'd invited him here, and she'd never hear the end of it.

"Leah, sit." Her mother slid into her own chair at the foot of the table. "Let us have prayer, and then everyone can eat before the food is ruined. I've just put more scrapple on to fry. You can turn that and then pour the coffee." Mam wiped her hands on her apron and smiled at Daniel. "You eat scrapple, don't you?"

His pleasant face creased in a smile. "Yes, Mrs. Yoder, I do. I love it, but I never get it anywhere but Pennsylvania, Delaware, or Ohio."

"Mam made it," Susanna chimed in. "I helped."

"Ya." Now that his pancakes were only a prayer away, Irwin's attitude softened. "It's *goot.*" He looked at Mam. "Can I go with Leah and the girls to see Daniel's show?"

Mam put her finger to her lips to signal silence. Everyone at the table, including Daniel, closed their eyes and offered silent thanks for the food and for the promise of the coming day. But when a moment had passed, Mam surprised them by saying, "Maybe our guest would like to say grace. I believe it is the Mennonite custom."

Leah looked at Daniel. He squirmed, cleared his throat and said, "Thank you, Lord, for family, community and new friends. And bless the hands that made this meal. Amen."

Grossmama grunted and reached for the syrup. "That was *goot*," she admitted. "A *goot* prayer."

"It was." Aunt Jezebel's eyes twinkled. "A *good* prayer. Thank you, Daniel."

Soon, everyone was too busy eating to talk or to stare at their visitor. Leah had been hungry when she'd awakened, but now, she found Mam's usually delicious pancakes tasted like dry fodder. She pushed a forkful around on her plate and sneaked a glance at Daniel, who was eating heartily.

"Leah," Mam reminded. "The scrapple?"

She leaped up, smelling the first whiff of something burning. "I forgot," she said, hurrying to the range to flip the crispy slabs. "Just in time." Using a hot mitt, she pushed the cast-iron frying pan back to a cooler section of the stovetop. It would soon be too warm to use the woodstove until fall, but Mam always said that the old stove cooked better than the modern gas one that stood beside it.

With something to do with her hands, it was easier for Leah to act as if a Mennonite boy came to breakfast every Sunday. What was wrong with her this morning? She was as giddy as a teenager. If she didn't gather her wits, Daniel would be sorry he'd come.

As Leah filled coffee cups around the table, she managed to get a good look at Daniel. She'd spent hours with him the night before, but in the dark, she really hadn't been able to see him clearly. He did look a little English in his white, button-up shirt and brown dress trousers, but there was something Dutch about him as well. Daniel had a pleasant face, good straight teeth that showed when he smiled and a fair complexion with ruddy cheeks. His thick brown hair was cut a little short for an Amish man, but what attracted her most were his unusually green eyes—even more striking than she remembered.

"Will you stop staring at him and give me some coffee?" *Grossmama* asked in the Amish dialect that the family usually spoke among themselves.

Mam's mouth firmed, and she looked directly at her mother-in-law. This was Mam's home and her kitchen, and she'd invited Daniel to eat with them. One of Mam's rules in this house was not to speak German in front of the English, because she felt it was rude.

Leah's insides clenched. Her grandmother had no call to embarrass her in front of Daniel—

hopefully he didn't understand Pennsylvania Dutch. But Rebecca giggled, and Susanna's mouth dropped open as she stared at Leah.

"Why's Leah starin' at Daniel?" Susanna asked, also in Dutch.

"She wants to make sure he has enough to eat," Mam supplied. "Leah, bring Daniel some of that scrapple."

"Danke," he said. *"Wunderbar."*

Leah's eyes widened. "You speak Pennsylvania Dutch?"

"Not very well, I'm afraid." He shrugged. "My grandfather spoke it when I was a child. I think I've forgotten most of what he taught me."

Hannah smiled. "But you probably understand a great deal."

"Ya," he replied.

Leah glanced at *Grossmama*, who had suddenly taken a great interest in her breakfast, and then back at Daniel.

He laid his fork down, wiped his mouth with a napkin and looked up at her. "Can you come this evening? Do you think the young people can come back as well? I thought tonight might be too soon for people to make arrangements, but it's the only night the Grange is free until Wednesday."

"You'll have to ask my daughter and son-in-law," Mam said. "They're the sponsors for the Gleaners. And, of course, it's up to the parents."

"We already got permission from the bishop," Rebecca reminded her. "For the kids to come last night."

"Aunt Mildred said that this wasn't a church Sunday for you," Daniel continued. "I promise not to keep the Gleaners up late. I think they'd enjoy the PowerPoint part of the program. Most people love the pictures of the camels. I know tomorrow's a school day, so my aunt has volunteered to pick everyone up in her van."

Irwin held up his plate for scrapple. "School's out for the summer in a week," he said. "I can't wait." Leah put two slices on his plate, and he slid them into a mountain of homemade catsup. "Can I go, Hannah? Can I go with Leah?"

Hannah shook her head. "*Ne*, Irwin. You are not old enough to be a Gleaner. Next year, when you're fourteen. The bishop said, 'No children.' He only gave permission for the teenagers."

"But I'm thirteen," Irwin protested. "I should be—"

Hannah gave him a *look*. Irwin's face fell, but he held his tongue. Leah was glad. Irwin was a normal boy who sometimes got sassy, but she didn't want him to make Mam look bad by arguing with her when they had a stranger at the table. Irwin continued to eat in silence, but the fact that he didn't run from the table in tears proved that he was gaining a little maturity.

"Will you be leaving Seven Poplars tomorrow?" Mam asked Daniel.

He shook his head. "No, Mrs. Yoder. I'm staying on at my aunt's for a few weeks until I get my next assignment."

"Assignment?" Leah's curiosity got the best of her, and the question popped out before she'd thought better of it. Daniel had just come back to the United States. Was he leaving again so soon? Disappointment washed over her. Other than finding Joey safe and sound, meeting Daniel had been the most exciting thing that had happened to her since she'd come home, and she'd hoped to continue the new friendship.

He nodded. "My parents, younger brother and younger sisters are living on an Indian reservation in Canada—my parents teach there. They've recently made the move from Spain, where I lived with them, but now I'm on my own."

"Do you get to pick where you go?" Mam asked.

"Sometimes," Daniel replied. "But I've asked to serve where I'm most needed."

"Could they send you back to Spain?" Leah asked.

"That's possible. At least I speak the language. But I could be assigned here in the States as well—anywhere from Appalachia to an inner-city community. Or they could send me as far away as Ukraine."

Leah put the serving plate back on the counter and returned to her seat at the table. "Won't you miss your family?" she asked him. "If you go far away?" She remembered how strange it had seemed at first when she'd gone to Ohio to tend to her grandmother. She'd been terribly home-sick, and she'd had her sister Rebecca for company.

"I will," Daniel said, grimacing. "That's the hard part about serving at an overseas mission. You're so isolated from family and friends you care about most. But I feel that the Lord has called me to help people who need it. There are lots of places where there's a real need for medical services. I'm not a doctor, but I am a nurse, and I think I can make a difference."

"So, as a nurse, you get to see other places and customs while you're doing God's work." Mam nodded. "Many Mennonite families are called to go on mission, but it can be hard on the children."

"My eldest sister, Margie, would agree with you, Mrs. Yoder. She married a Methodist dentist and lives in a small town in Nebraska. She says she has no intentions of moving again—ever."

"Call me *Hannah*, please," Mam said gently. "We Amish don't use fancy titles."

"I'm sorry," Daniel said. "I didn't—"

"Ne," Grossmama interjected. "It is not the *Plain* way."

"Just *Hannah* will do fine," Mam said. "As to whether or not the young people may go to hear tonight's program, I think the best thing would be for you to go down to my son-in-law Charley's house. Leah can show you the way."

"I'll just help clear the table first," she said.

"Ne, no need." Mam sipped her coffee. "There are plenty of hands to make short work of the breakfast dishes. You go on with Daniel."

"Irwin can point out Miriam and Charley's house," *Grossmama* said. "It's just across the field."

"I don't mind." Leah rose, wiping her mouth with a paper napkin. "I wanted to take some of that scrapple to Miriam anyway. You know it's her favorite."

Taking the hint, Daniel murmured his thanks for breakfast, said his goodbyes while she made a plate of scrapple, and then followed her outside into the yard. His truck was parked in the driveway.

"Did you want to drive over or should we walk?" he asked.

Leah caught a glimpse of someone pulling

aside a kitchen curtain and waved as Susanna's round little face appeared, pressed against the glass. Her sister waved furiously before abruptly disappearing. Probably Mam had seen her peeking out the window and pulled her away. One thing about having a big family—someone was always watching.

"Leah?" Daniel looked hesitant. "I'd be glad to drive you, if it isn't against the rules for you to ride with me."

She looked at him in disbelief. "Why wouldn't I be able to ride in your truck? I'm Amish, not Muslim."

His ruddy cheeks grew even redder. "I didn't know. I already did the wrong thing inside—by calling your mother Mrs. Yoder. I didn't want to get you into trouble." He reached over and opened the cab door.

Leah smiled at him. "Don't worry. I doubt if Mam was shocked. She used to be Mennonite, you know—before she married my father. She converted to Amish for him."

"Oh." Daniel walked around the front of the pickup and got behind the wheel. "So, what you're saying is that your mother isn't as strict?"

Leah chuckled, setting the plate covered with foil on her lap. "No, I didn't say that at all. Delaware Amish are very *Old Order*—very traditional—and my mother is a faithful member of the church. It's just that few people, other than my grandmother, would object to my riding down our lane to my sisters' house. We won't even have to go out on the blacktop road. It's not as though we were going to Ocean City, to the boardwalk." She stopped, suddenly feeling very silly. "Not that we would—that you would. I was...was just saying."

Daniel smiled at her. "I think that you are a unique young woman, Leah Yoder. And with me, you can say whatever you like."

Leah smiled back as her awkward moment slid away. It was hard to remain on edge around Daniel. He was just so...so nice. He made her feel happy, just being near him. "I wanted to hear your talk last night," she said. "And now that I know you a little better, I'm even more eager to hear about your experiences. It's something I've always admired, spreading God's word." She pointed. "Go that way, around the barn."

"I don't know if I've led anyone to the Lord," he answered as he turned the key and drove slowly out of the farmyard.

"What about that boy you saved from the mob in Morocco?"

"Mousa?" Daniel chuckled again. "That rascal? It turned out that he was innocent of the theft that almost got him killed, but I'm afraid that he's still...um...a work in progress."

"Mou-sa? His name is Mou-sa? What happened to him? He must have been grateful that you saved his life."

Daniel shrugged. "I'll explain it all during my program, or at least a shortened version of *life as Mousa sees it.*"

"But you kept him safe, didn't you?"

Daniel eased the truck around the barn and corncrib. "After I brought him home, it was impossible to reform him, and even more impossible to make a convert of him. When he claimed to be a homeless orphan, my father found a respectable foster family for him and paid for his tuition at a private school out of his own pocket."

"And?" Leah was intrigued.

"He ran away from the foster home and the school about a dozen times. Turns out, Mousa wasn't an orphan. He had a father and a mother and nine brothers—all of whom made their living by hoodwinking well-meaning foreigners."

"How terrible. Was your father angry?"

"Not really. Perhaps angry with himself for not investigating the situation further. But these things happen. We can't not offer aid just because someone might occasionally take advantage of us."

"I suppose that makes sense. There's the farmhouse." Leah pointed. "It's new. The community pitched in to build it last summer when Ruth and Eli got married."

"But I thought you said that Charley and Miriam lived here."

Leah laughed. "They do. Ruth and Eli live in the bottom part of the house. Charley and Miriam have the top floor. It works out great because Miriam is good with animals and can't make toast without burning it."

"And Ruth, I suppose, cooks like your mother."

"Exactly." He drove slowly down the narrow dirt road that led to the little farmhouse. "And what about you? Are you a fabulous cook?"

She smiled back. "I'm learning. I have to admit, I'm a better seamstress than a cook."

"I don't cook at all. My mother kept trying to tell me that I might have to cook for myself, but I was always too busy to learn. And I had three sisters. They're notorious for spoiling brothers."

"I wouldn't know about that," she replied. "I only have sisters—six of them."

"More than me. I only have three sisters and two brothers, but they're all special."

"I'm sure they are," Leah said. *They must be, if they're anything like you.* Suddenly, she felt as though she'd known Daniel all her life. What was there about him that made him so easy to talk to? If only he was Amish, she thought.

If only...

Chapter Six

For nearly an hour, Leah sat motionless in her chair, her eyes fixed on the screen as Daniel led his audience through the narrow alleys and bazaars of foreign cities with names that rolled off his tongue as sweet and sour as Aunt Fannie's chow-chow. It was nearly impossible for her to keep from weeping as Daniel's pictures showed the plight of ragged, beggar children, or the ill-fed and overburdened horses and donkeys that fought for space on the crowded streets among the honking flood of dilapidated cars and trucks.

And if the pitiful sights touched Leah's heart and soul, so too did the hopeful scenes of the clinic where Daniel had assisted volunteer doctors and midwives in offering free medical care to the poor. Equally inspiring was the orphanage and school that the Mennonites supported to provide for homeless children, lost souls who otherwise might have turned to crime to survive.

"In Morocco, we are not allowed to preach or offer any public worship services," Daniel explained. "Instead, we try to do what good we can in the Lord's name and attempt to influence people by example."

He paused for a short break when the talk moved from Morocco to Spain. There, life was much freer for missionaries; they were permitted to move around the country, preach the Gospel, offer educational programs and teach in the schools. Leah was fascinated by the old buildings, the parks and gardens, and the slides of farms, scenic mountains and ocean beaches. Daniel said that he'd liked the Spanish people and had been impressed by their loyalty to family and the sense of history and culture that held a place in every part of their lives.

When the lights came on and Daniel thanked everyone for coming, it took a few seconds for Leah to realize that Susanna was chattering away to her. So absolute was her concentration on Daniel's world that Miriam had to take hold of her arm before she broke out of her reverie.

"Did you fall asleep?" Miriam asked, teasingly.

"Lemonade," Susanna repeated. "Pink. Want some?"

Leah met her little sister's excited gaze. "No.

You go on with Miriam." As the two followed Charley and the Gleaners to the refreshment table, Leah found herself drawn to the desk where Daniel was shutting down his laptop.

"Daniel?"

He glanced up and his face creased in a big smile. "Leah. I hope I didn't waste your evening."

"No." She shook her head. "It was wonderful. *You* were wonderful."

His green eyes lit up with pleasure. "I'm glad." He shrugged modestly. "I tend to run on. Speaking's not really my strong suit. I like the work... What I mean is, this speaking thing wasn't my idea. But Douglas Wheeler—he's on the mission board—thought that because I'm younger than most of our speakers and not a pastor that I might attract more teenagers to..." He stopped and chuckled. "There I go again. I told you, I talk too much."

"I don't think so," she said, smiling back at him. "I think you're...inspiring."

"It's nice of you to say so." He hesitated, carefully wrapping up an electrical cord. "I wondered..."

"Yes?"

Daniel cleared his throat and grimaced, for just a moment looking more like fifteen than however old he really was. "I don't know if you'd be interested, or if it's allowed, but on Tuesday,

Caroline, Leslie and I are helping out at the food bank in Dover. It's only open once a week. My aunt usually volunteers there, but she's having a root canal. Do you think—"

"I'd like to help?" Leah suggested. "I would. Very much."

"That's great. It wouldn't be a problem for you, would it? I mean, your church doesn't usually allow you to do volunteer work for outsiders."

"That's true," she said, never having thought about it that way before. "But that doesn't apply to me because I haven't joined the Amish church yet. I'm allowed to do what I want." Leah chuckled. "Within reason. And I think that helping out at the food bank would be something I'd like to do."

"Great." He laughed. "I said that before, didn't I?"

"It's all right." She suddenly felt shy. "I don't mind."

"I think I like you, Leah Yoder."

She glanced up into his pleasant face and, for a moment, felt giddy, as if the floor had suddenly swayed under her feet. "And I think I like you, Daniel Brown."

"Good." His crooked smile widened. "The girls and I will pick you up at twelve-thirty on Tuesday, if that's okay?" She nodded and he went on. "And wear comfortable shoes. You won't get a chance to sit down until our shift ends at five."

The kitchen clock was striking nine-thirty when Leah, Susanna and Rebecca arrived home to find Mam and Aunt Jezebel waiting up for them. "Oh, you should have come with us!" Leah exclaimed. "It was wonderful! The pictures of Spain and Morocco were beautiful! And Daniel…Daniel is just—"

"Goot!" Susanna said, bouncing from foot to foot. "I saw camels and monkeys. Silly monkeys."

Rebecca nodded. "It was fun. And Miriam and Charley agreed it was educational for the young people. The kids loved it, and even Herman Beachy was on his best behavior."

"Daniel's a wonderful speaker," Leah added. "When he talks about the desert or the noisy marketplace, he makes you feel as though you're right there, smelling the spices and hearing the clamor of the crowded streets."

"It sounds as if they had a good time." Aunt Jezebel's voice was breathy and soft. She hesitated before asking, "There was no preaching the Mennonite faith at the talk, was there?"

"Ne," Rebecca assured her. "Even Bishop Atlee would have approved of tonight's program."

"I'm glad," Mam said with a smile. "It's good for you to see something of the outside."

"But I wouldn't want to live like that—like Daniel and his family," Rebecca said. "In some foreign place where we wouldn't know anyone and everything was strange."

"*Ya,* the Mennonites differ from us," her mother said. "They feel called to spread the word of God, while we Amish believe the Lord has instructed us to live apart from the world."

Susanna wrinkled her nose and tugged on her mother's sleeve. "I want a camel. With a hump. I like camels."

"No camels." Mam sighed. "The feed store doesn't sell camel chow. We'll have to make do with horses and cows."

Aunt Jezebel's eyes twinkled. "*Ya,* Susanna, what would the bishop think if we hitched a camel to our buggy instead of a horse?"

Leah laughed. Aunt Jezzy was always more fun after *Grossmama* went to bed. Her shy aunt had a real sense of humor. The two older women had spent years living under the same roof, and as uncharitable as it might be to judge, Leah felt that *Grossmama* often bullied and was unkind to her younger sister. Aunt Jezebel always seemed happier on the days that *Grossmama* went to the senior center.

"Camels are not *Plain*," Rebecca said with a giggle.

"Ne," Mam agreed solemnly. "Definitely not *Plain*." And then they all laughed.

Leah went to the window and pulled aside the curtain. Daniel's Aunt Joyce's van was gone. She hadn't expected to still see him there, but still, the dark yard left her with a sense of longing. "Daniel drove us home," she said.

"Home," Susanna echoed, her word nearly lost in a yawn.

"Bedtime for you, sleepyhead," Mam said. "Time we all turned in, I think."

Leah nodded. Three mornings a week, *Grossmama* was picked up to go to Maple Leaf, the Englisher senior center, where she taught other women how to make beautiful braided rugs. On those days, Leah went to help Anna with the children and housework. Leah was naturally an early riser, so being at Anna's by seven a.m. was not a problem. Usually, she would sit up until at least ten, doing puzzles with her sisters or listening to Rebecca read news from the *Budget*. But tonight, as much as she loved being with her family, Leah wanted to be alone.

She wanted to climb into bed and think about all she'd seen and heard.

She wanted to remember how Daniel's face had seemed to glow with an inner light when he'd told about the work of the Mennonite missionaries in faraway places where impoverished people lived difficult lives and had to struggle to find enough to eat. He wasn't preachy, but when he spoke, she could feel his honesty and dedication to serving God. And maybe, most of all, she wanted to remember how he'd smiled when he said he liked her.

Being part of a tight-knit Amish community, Leah had always been involved in hands-on sharing days, sewing bees and school fund-raising auctions. But none of those efforts seemed as worthwhile or as exciting as what Daniel was doing, and she couldn't help wishing that her church could reach out to help strangers.

As everyone made final preparations for bed, Leah let Jeremiah, Irwin's little terrier, outside to relieve himself. Mam had gotten her share of disapproving looks from her neighbors for permitting a dog to sleep in the house instead of in the barn with Flora, the family's sheepdog, but Mam had stood her ground. Irwin had been a lost and troubled boy, and Jeremiah an abandoned mutt. The two had bonded from the first day that Leah's sister, Ruth, had carried the starving pup home, and Mam insisted that Jeremiah and Irwin had healed each other. Usually, Jeremiah curled up at the foot of Irwin's bed, but tonight Irwin was spending the night with his Beachy cousins, and it fell to Leah to see to the terrier's needs.

"Don't take all night," Leah called to the little dog. It was very dark, with only a few stars piercing the heavy cloud cover. She thought that it might rain again this evening. In the west, she caught sight of a flash of lightning. "Jeremiah!" Leah called. "Come on!"

The kitchen door squeaked and Leah's mother stepped out on the porch beside her. She didn't have to turn to see who it was, and Mam didn't need to speak to be recognized. There was no mistaking the scent of lavender soap that Mam favored.

"Daniel asked me if I wanted to help at the Mennonite Food Bank in Dover on Tuesday afternoon. Caroline and Leslie Steiner will be there." Leah hesitated. "I told him I would, and he's going to pick me up after lunch."

"I see."

When silence stretched between them, Leah called for the dog again and then said, "He must be chasing a mouse or one of the cats."

"He'll come when he's ready," Mam said. "I wanted a minute alone with you. It seems that my instincts were right." Soft fingertips brushed Leah's chin. "You find Daniel Brown attractive, don't you?"

"Daniel?"

Her mother chuckled. "He is a nice young man." Her voice grew more serious. "But he's not for you, Leah. He's not one of us."

"I went to see his program," she defended. "And I'm helping to give out food to people who need it. I'm not walking out with him."

"*Ne,* you're not, but you've imagined what it might be like, haven't you?"

Leah didn't answer. She wasn't ready to admit to Mam or even to herself that the attraction she felt for Daniel was different…stronger than for any of the boys with whom she'd grown up. Instead, she called for Jeremiah again. Still no ragged little black-and-white dog with a silly plumed tail. "Where can he have gotten to?"

"Leah."

She sighed. "I know he's Mennonite, Mam, but it doesn't hurt to think what might be, does it?"

Her mother's hand closed around hers. "It is your running around time, and it's only right that you see how others live, but don't look too far. It could make you unhappy when you choose the *Plain* life."

"It's not like I'm smoking cigarettes or making a show of myself with the English boys at Spence's. I'm going to be helping those less fortunate, families in need. Is that so wrong?"

"No, not wrong, but dangerous all the same."

Her shoulders stiffened. "Are you forbidding me to go?"

"*Ne,* child. That's not my place. You're a woman grown."

Again, Leah couldn't answer. Would she have gone anyway if her mother told her not to? She suspected that she might.

Mam's voice took on a thread of steel. "Have you never wondered about my other family? My mother? My father? My sisters and brothers?"

"Ruth used to ask when we were kids, but you told us that was in the past. We were your family then and now."

Mam squeezed her hand. "I should have been honest when Ruth asked, but it was still too hurtful for me. I was weak, and it was easier not to talk about them. I'm afraid I'm a work in progress. You don't know how many nights I've gone on my knees praying for the strength to be a good mother."

"But you are," Leah said. "No one could have a better one."

"That's sweet of you to say, but—"

"It's how I feel, Mam—how we all feel."

"Thank you for telling me. But now, I need you to listen."

"I am."

Mam nodded. "When I married your father and joined the Amish church, it broke my father's heart. My grandmother closed the door in my face, and my father forbade me to come home. He returned the letters I wrote to my sisters and mother, unopened."

"Oh, Mam." Leah hugged her. "It must have been awful for you. Why didn't you tell us?"

"I never wanted you children to feel that I was sorry for the decision I made. I've never regretted it, not for a moment. But that doesn't mean that I don't miss my old family, that I didn't want to see you in my mother's arms. You look like her, you know. She was fair of face and beautiful in spirit."

Leah felt her cheeks flame. All her life, she'd known that other people considered her pretty, but it wasn't something that the *Plain* folk were supposed to remark on, or that she was supposed to take pride in. Pride was *Hochmut*. Forbidden. It was against the *Ordnung*, the laws that governed every aspect of Amish life.

"Your mother turned her back on you after you married Dat?" Leah looked at Mam. "How could she?"

"She had no choice. In our home, my father's word was final. He was ordained, a leader in our church. By leaving our faith for Jonas's church, my father felt that I had rejected him and shamed him before the members of his community. My mother was raised among the Old Order Mennonite, and it would have been unthinkable for her to go against her husband."

"Did you know…before? That they would disown you if you married Dat?"

"*Ya.* My oldest brother enlisted in the military. His name was Timothy. He was funny and kind, and he always had time to listen to my chatter. He taught me to bait a fishhook and to ride a horse bareback. I adored Tim. I was twelve the last time I saw him."

"I have an uncle who's a soldier?"

Her mother made a small sound that was almost a sob. "Tim came home once, after he graduated from basic training. My father wouldn't let him see my mother—see any of us. Tim hitched a ride with another serviceman back to their duty station. There was an accident on the interstate."

"He was killed?" Leah asked.

Her mother nodded. "Both of them were. They told us that that they found alcohol in the wreck—that the boys had been drinking. My father refused to allow Tim to be buried in our cemetery. He told the soldiers who came to notify us of Tim's passing that he had no son."

"Dat would never do that," Leah protested. Tears clouded her vision. "No matter what we did, he'd never have denied one of us."

"*Ne,*" her mother said. "I don't believe that he

would. But you're of an age when you'll make decisions that will affect the rest of your life. You have to realize that you are Amish, blood and bone. Nothing will ever change that."

"But I'm free to choose, am I not?" She laid her hand on the porch rail and looked into the darkness. "Isn't that part of our faith?"

"It is. Joining the church, making the commitment to live a *Plain* life is a decision we must each make for ourselves. You're past the age most girls have already been baptized, and I wouldn't be honest if I didn't tell you I was concerned that you have doubts."

"Not doubts, not really. I just…" Leah searched for the right words to explain her restlessness to her mother…to tell her in a way that wouldn't involve Daniel. "I want to be sure," she said, and that much was true. She'd felt this way all her life, as though she belonged…but didn't.

"And so you should be. Just remember, if you chose not to be one of us, you give up everything you've ever known."

"Not my family. You wouldn't stop loving me, would you, Mam?"

"*Ne,* child, never. I want you to be happy, but I also want you to be realistic. And I want you to realize that if you chose a husband from outside our faith, many of your larger family—friends, relatives, neighbors would be lost to you."

"I know that…but I don't know why you're saying this to me. I'm not dating anyone, and—"

"Hush, Leah. Don't say what you'll regret. We've always known each other's hearts. You may look like my mother, but you're a lot like me. There's an independence in you that your sisters don't share. You'll follow your heart, no matter where it leads you." She took a deep breath. "I'm just saying that your life will be a lot simpler if you find a nice Amish boy and start walking out with him."

"Do you have anyone in mind?" Leah went to the steps and whistled for Jeremiah. "I've a mind to leave him out all night."

Her mother joined her. "I wouldn't have you think that your grandfather was a bad man. He wasn't. He was a good man. He loved his children, and we loved him. But he was very set in his ways. My mother always said that Dad would have been a martyr if he'd lived in the bad times in Germany."

Leah stepped back and looked into her mother's face. It was dark on the porch, and her features were hidden in shadow. "So you knew the price you'd have to pay, but you chose to follow your heart and marry Dat."

"*Ya,* I did. For me, I think it was the right choice. I could never have had a better husband—a better father for my children." She sighed. "Maybe I took after my Dad…maybe I'm as stubborn as he was."

"But you wouldn't—" Jeremiah began to bark. "What's wrong with him?"

"I think someone's coming," her mother said. "There." She pointed.

Leah stared into the darkness and saw a small beam of light. "Who'd be coming this late? On foot?"

Chapter Seven

"We'll see, won't we?" Mam started down the steps.

"Wait," Leah cautioned. "Let me get a flashlight."

"Hello!" Mam called.

"It's me! Johanna." The flashlight beam bobbed and grew brighter. Jeremiah's excited yips nearly drowned out her sister's voice.

"Johanna?" Leah called. "Is someone sick?" She hurried down the steps after her mother. She couldn't imagine why her eldest sister had walked over in the dark this late at night.

"We're all fine," Johanna answered. But something in her voice told Leah that wasn't quite true.

Leah's nephew, red-haired Jonah, ran into her mother's arms and Mam scooped him up. "How's my big boy?" she asked. "Did you walk all the way over here?"

"Ya," Jonah said shyly. "I did. Katy rode."

Leah heard the squeak of wagon wheels and Johanna materialized out of the dark, pulling Jonah's little red wagon. Katy, the baby, sprawled inside, one small booted foot hanging over the wooden railing.

"Not so far," Johanna said. "We took a short-cut through the fields, came down the woods lane and up through your pasture."

It was still a long way for a four-year-old to walk and her sister to pull the baby. "Is she asleep?" She hugged Johanna. "I wish I'd known you wanted to come. I'd have hitched up one of the horses and driven over to fetch you."

"Too bad we don't have one of those cell phones," Johanna said, switching off her flashlight and putting it in the wagon. "But it didn't take me long. Katy's sleeping like a log. It's way past her bedtime."

Leah looked at her, waiting for some explanation.

"Wilmer's not at home, and Jonah and I decided that it would be fun to spend the night with all of you," Johanna said.

"Wilmer took the horse and buggy?" Mam asked. Leah could tell by her mother's tone that she was suspicious, too. This simply wasn't a spur-of-the-moment decision to come visiting, but Johanna would tell them the real reason when she was good and ready.

"*Ya,* he did. I don't expect him home tonight, and we got lonely for company, didn't we, Jonah?" Johanna said with forced joviality. She lifted Katy, still sleeping and clutching her beloved rag doll, out of the wagon and cradled her against one shoulder. "Has everyone else gone to bed?"

"I think so," Mam replied. "But we've always got room for you. Leah can take Jonah to bed with her, and you can sleep with me."

"I think there's some rhubarb pie left," Leah said. She knew that Johanna was partial to rhubarb.

"That and a glass of buttermilk would hit the spot," her sister murmured.

"Well, don't just stand there," Mam said. "Let's get these little ones into the house and into bed. Thank goodness I've got that crib still set up in the corner of my bedroom."

Johanna and Leah glanced at each other and laughed. Mam had had that crib there as long as either of them could remember. It was always useful for visiting grandchildren or neighbors' babies or for church services when the whole congregation came for the day. The quilts and sheets changed over the years, but they were always kept fresh and clean, and Leah had lost track of the number of babies who had slept in it.

Inside, they found that Rebecca, Susanna and Aunt Jezebel had gone on to bed. Someone had turned off the propane lamp, leaving just the antique kerosene lantern burning on the kitchen table. Mam passed Jonah to Leah. "Give his face and hands a lick and a promise and tuck him in while we put Katy to bed. Then we'll all have some of that pie and buttermilk."

Jonah's eyes were heavy-lidded and it was clear to see that he was on the verge of falling asleep. "Let's just get this hat and jacket off you," Leah said. "Aunt Rebecca's already in bed. Let's surprise her."

"Go with your Aunt Leah like a big boy," Johanna said to the child. "And in the morning, I'll make you something special for breakfast."

Jonas murmured something and Leah carried him upstairs, first to the bathroom, and then to the bedroom she shared with Rebecca. Her sister had left a lamp burning, and she sat up when Leah entered the room. "Who have you got there?" she asked teasingly. "It can't be our Jonah."

"Ya." He yawned. "It's Jonah."

Rebecca met Leah's gaze, obviously curious, but Leah shrugged. "Johanna brought the chil-

dren to spend the night with us," she said. "I suppose we'll know why in the morning. Or not."

Rebecca put out her arms, and Leah tucked
him in under the quilt beside her sister. The boy's
curly hair, exactly the same shade as Rebecca's,
mingled with hers on the white pillowcase. "He
smells sweet," Leah said. "Like pumpkin pie."

"Do not," Jonah said, but he giggled sleepily.

Leah smiled at him. He was an adorable child,
good-natured, and independent, for four. Whenever she saw Jonah, she couldn't help thinking
what it would be like to have a little boy or girl
just like him someday. "Make sure he says his
prayers," she reminded Rebecca. And then she
blew out the lamp and made her way back downstairs in the semidarkness.

As she neared the kitchen doorway, Leah
heard Johanna say, "I pray for him, Mam. I think
his is a troubled soul."

Leah couldn't make out Mam's reply, but it
was obvious that her mother was concerned. As
she entered the room, Johanna broke off in mid-
sentence and glanced at her. That was when Leah
saw the large purple bruise on her sister's left
cheekbone.

Leah's chest tightened. "How did you get that
bruise on your face?" she demanded, but she had
a sinking feeling that she already knew.

Her sister's marriage to moody Wilmer Detweiler had been a rocky one from the start, and Leah could never understand why Johanna had accepted his proposal. The church taught that members of a congregation were all one family and should love each other like brothers and sisters, but Leah had never taken to Wilmer.

From the first, Johanna and Wilmer had struggled financially, and difficult pregnancies with both children put even more strain on the relationship. On several occasions, there had been discord, followed by disturbing incidents between Johanna and Wilmer, such as Wilmer's public complaints about his wife and his rough-handedness with her. It was a sensitive subject, because marital relationships were considered private, to be kept within the home, and Johanna never complained.

A husband was expected to be the head of the family, to command respect, but physical abuse directed toward a wife—toward anyone—was not permitted by the Amish. A marriage was supposed to be a partnership. Any type of violence went against their teachings.

Shamed by the difficulties between her and her husband, Johanna had tried to hide her injuries. Eventually, Mam had found out and confronted Wilmer. And when he rejected her intervention, Mam had reported Johanna's plight to the elders of the church. Samuel, as deacon, and other members of the congregation had taken him to task, and the family had hoped that the trouble was in the past.

But if Wilmer had struck Johanna again, the old problems had resurfaced, making Leah frightened for her sister's safety. "Was it Wilmer?" Leah asked. "Did he hit you?"

"Ne, an accident." Johanna averted her gaze, making Leah certain that her sister was protecting her husband.

Unconsciously, Leah's fingers balled into fists at her sides. This wasn't the fun-loving and confident big sister she'd always counted on. Leah's heart ached for her. "Oh, Johanna," she said. "How could he?"

"I said it was an accident," her sister repeated. "I was getting some jars of peaches out of the cupboard and one fell and…" She looked up through moist lashes. "Just peaches," she finished softly.

"Peaches, my foot!" Leah threw her arms around Johanna and hugged her tightly. "We should call the police. Wilmer should be locked up."

"Ne, ne." Johanna pulled out of Leah's embrace, covered her face with her hands, and began to sob. "No English." She shook her head. "No police. It's not our way."

"She's right," Mam put in. "We do not involve the English in our troubles."

"But we've tried *our* way," Leah argued. "Wilmer promised that it would never happen again. And now it has!"

"Hush." Mam raised a finger to her lips. "This is Johanna's business. Best you not trouble her further tonight. She's here with us, and she's safe—"

"Until morning!" Leah retorted. "And then what? Wilmer will come for her, and she'll go with him like the last time?"

"He will be better tomorrow," Johanna said. "It was his headache again. Katy has been fussy all day, and Wilmer couldn't sleep. He has terrible headaches. I know not to vex him when he's in pain, but I lost my temper when he scolded Jonah for spilling his milk. It was my fault. It's a father's duty to teach his children proper behavior."

"You can't go on making excuses for him," Leah said. She couldn't take her gaze off Johanna's hands. Although her sister had only recently turned twenty-five, her slender hands were red and calloused from doing hard labor and looked as though they belonged to a much older woman. "We'll send word to Samuel and the church elders," Leah insisted. "They'll—"

"Ne." Johanna shook her head even harder.

"If you shame Wilmer, it will be worse for me and the children. Pray for him. He's a good man weighed down by ill health and misfortune."

"I don't think he is a good man." Leah's words came out in a rush. "I think he's lazy—and a bully."

"Enough, Leah," Mam said. "Maybe you should go on to bed. Praying for Wilmer would be the best thing you can do for Johanna and for the children right now. God's power to change hearts is greater than ours."

"Mam, we're past the point of prayer. Your daughter and grandchildren are in danger. Why are you not more upset about this?" Leah settled her hands on her hips. "She should leave him and come home for good."

Johanna wiped the tears from her face. "He is my husband, Leah. If I leave the marriage, I break a contract I made before God. We're not English. I cannot break up a family because we have differences."

"Differences?" Leah motioned to the bruise on Johanna's cheek. "What would you do if he struck Katy like that? Would you stand by and watch him do her permanent harm?"

"Wilmer's never laid a hand on Katy in anger," Johanna said. "You should know I would never allow my children to remain in danger. As for me, I can take care of myself. And it's unfair to call him lazy. His trade is a hard one, especially in bad weather."

"I'm sure he is a good carpenter—when he works," Leah said. "How many days was he off this past winter?"

"Construction is slow. It's not Wilmer's fault if—"

"It's his fault if he's home and still abed while you're out feeding the sheep and turkeys. Or hoeing the garden. Lots of Amish men work forty hours outside the home and then come home and tend the farm. Wilmer leaves the house, the bees, the poultry and the livestock to you. Not to mention the quilts you sew or the canned jams and jellies you sell to the English."

"Leah." Her mother's tone grew sharp. "I won't ask you again to leave us. You're not helping your sister. She needs time to think, to decide for herself the right thing to do. You cannot make such decisions for her, and neither can I. You're young. You don't—"

"I may be young, but I know right from wrong," Leah insisted. "I think Wilmer's dangerous, and I couldn't bear it if anything happened to Johanna or either of the children."

"None of us could," her mother said.

Leah sighed and hung her head. "I'm sorry, Mam. I didn't mean to be disrespectful to you."

"I know you didn't," Mam said. "We'll talk in

the morning, after Johanna has had time to pray and to consider her options."

"All right." Swallowing the arguments she wanted to make, Leah left the kitchen and started up the wide stairs to her bedroom. But the unspoken words echoed in her mind. *What Wilmer's doing is wrong, and if neither of you will do anything to stop him, I will.*

But there was no time to speak to her mother about Johanna's abusive husband the following morning. Apparently, Mam and Johanna had stayed up late into the night, and Johanna and the baby were still sleeping in when the rest of the family gathered around the table for breakfast. This was *Grossmama*'s senior center day, and she was too excited to have more than a cup of black coffee before the bus arrived to pick her up.

"We have breakfast and lunch there," her grandmother said loudly. "On trays. Fruit and waffles, bacon and eggs. But not real eggs. They taste funny. And *decaffeinated* coffee." *Grossmama* wrinkled her nose in disgust. "What good is that? I make them give me tea." She scowled at Irwin. "Where are my bags?"

"On'na porch," the boy said.

The rug-making supplies that her grandmother was looking for were in two old-fash-

ioned carpet bags, and it was Irwin's job to lug
them out to the gate so that the driver could stow
them in the back of the bus. "Irwin carried them
out for you," Leah soothed. "Just as he always
does." She threw Irwin a sympathetic glance. He
ducked his head and slurped his milk.

"I don't trust him. Beachys all have sneaky
eyes."

"Irwin has the eyes God gave him," Mam said,
smiling at Irwin. "And they serve him well, now
that he has new glasses."

Grossmama scrunched up her face and picked
at the single black hair on her chin. "The bus is
late. It's always late."

"It's not time yet," Leah said. "The bus doesn't
come until seven-thirty."

Despite her complaints, Leah knew that her
grandmother enjoyed the experience because
she complained even more when the center was
closed for the holidays. Her grandmother was
the first Old Amish woman in Kent County to
attend a program for older English people. Anna
had been instrumental in convincing the church
elders that it was in *Grossmama*'s best interest
to allow her to attend Maple Leaf.

This was apparently one of her grandmother's good days, because, even though she was
grumbling, her fussing made sense. Of course,
Grossmama was always sharper in the morn-

ing. She rarely asked where Dat was before noon. He'd been her only son, and most days—although he'd been dead and buried for three years—*Grossmama* was positive that he was in the barn milking the cows and would be in any moment.

Leah poured coffee for her grandmother and found the black high-top athletic shoes and long black sports socks with the orange basketballs that her grandmother insisted on wearing to the center along with her traditional black dress, cape and bonnet.

"Have a good day," Leah said as she finished tying *Grossmama*'s shoelaces. "I have to go to Anna's now."

"Why isn't Anna here? It's not decent, an unmarried girl out of the house all night. She wasn't here at supper, either."

"Anna's in her husband's home," Leah reminded gently. "She married Samuel, and I'm going to help with the children and the washing."

"She has children already? Didn't take her much time, did it? As fat as she is, no wonder I didn't know she was in the family way." *Grossmama*'s mouth puckered. "If Hannah had kept a tighter rein on the girl, she wouldn't have had a baby so soon after her wedding."

Leah didn't attempt to explain that Anna and Samuel hadn't had any children yet or that

Samuel had been a widower with five children when they'd married, two months ago. She just smiled and hurried for the back door. As she passed Rebecca, she tugged at her sister's apron. "I won't be back until afternoon," she whispered. "Don't let Johanna leave the house."

"I'll do my best," Rebecca promised.

Mam glanced at them and raised an eyebrow.

"Have a good day in school," Leah called.

"I'm taking the buggy today, instead of walking," her mother said. "And I may be late getting home. You girls will have to start supper."

"We will," Leah replied. She wished she had a chance to give Rebecca more than a brief account of what she suspected had happened last night. She hadn't wanted to talk with Jonah in the bedroom. The child probably knew better than any of them what went on in his parents' home, but Leah couldn't add more grief to the child's lot.

Leah grabbed a scarf off the hook by the door and tied it over her hair. She had a *kapp* in her pocket, but the scarf would do for the walk across the field to Anna's. Because the morning would be hard work—house cleaning and washing clothes—she'd donned her patched but serviceable dark green dress and an old apron of Mam's. Leah wished this wasn't one of her Anna days, because she'd worry about Johanna until she got back. Maybe, if she skipped lunch, she might be finished with the day's chores by two, perhaps even earlier.

The delicious smell of cinnamon bread fresh out of the oven washed over Leah as she opened Anna's back door. "Aunt Leah!" squealed four-year-old Lori Ann as she flung herself at Leah's legs. "You're here!"

"Yes, I'm here." Leah laughed and unwound Lori Ann's arms from her knees.

"M...Mae wet the bed," Lori Ann proclaimed.

"But me sor-ry," her little sister shouted.

Samuel, a big, hearty man with a full dark brown beard and kind eyes, nodded, drained his coffee and bid Leah a good day. Leah knew that Samuel had probably been up since four a.m.— he looked tired and there were worry lines at the corners of his eyes.

"Is Samuel well?" Leah asked once her brother-in-law had gone outside. As she watched her sister kneading bread dough, it occurred to Leah that Anna didn't appear her usual calm and cheerful self, either.

"He didn't get much sleep last night," Anna confided. "Deacon business."

Naomi looked up from her book. "Wilmer was here," she said. "Talking with Dat."

Leah met Anna's gaze. Wilmer had come

here? Leah's thoughts raced as she tried to fill in the blanks. As deacon, it was Samuel's duty to see that all the members of the church community followed the rules and lived in harmony. He would have been the first one to chastise Johanna's husband for abusing her. So why had Wilmer come to Samuel? And what had Samuel done about it?

Chapter Eight

Anna pursed her lips and gently shook her head, warning Leah that they couldn't talk in front of the children. Turning to Naomi, Anna smiled and raised a flour-dusted finger to her lips. "*Ne,* my love. We don't tell who comes to talk with your father. A deacon's family must remember that church matters are to be kept private." She went to the table and gave her eight-year-old step-daughter a hug. "Now, if you want to be helpful, I could use your help packing the school lunches."

Naomi sighed, closed her book and rose to obey.

"Me help," little Mae chimed in.

"*Ya,*" Naomi agreed. "You can wash the apples."

It was difficult for Leah to curb her curiosity. She couldn't wait to discuss Johanna's plight with Anna after the older children left for school, but she knew that her sister was right, so she bit back her questions.

Naomi set her library book safely out of reach of her younger siblings and went to gather the black lunch pails that she and her twin brothers, Peter and Rudy, carried to school. As the girl efficiently began to assemble sandwiches, apples and muffins, Leah couldn't help noticing what a difference Anna had made in Naomi in the short time since the wedding. Already the child looked far better than she had before, happier and more attractive. Her shining hair was neatly braided under a starched *kapp*, and her new, rose-colored dress fit her perfectly.

Samuel had done his best for his five children after his wife had died, but the home needed a mother, and loving Anna filled that spot perfectly. It was clear to Leah that—despite the difference in Samuel and Anna's ages—the new marriage was off to a solid start. That Samuel would have courted Anna in the first place was a surprise to the community, but not to Leah. From the first, she'd seen real affection between the two, and Leah hoped that when she married, if she ever did, she'd find a man as good as Samuel to call husband.

She was about to ask Anna what time she'd gotten to bed, when Rudy, Peter and Samuel came back in and everyone gathered around the table for breakfast. Leah didn't get a chance to speak privately to Anna until the kids left for school and the two younger girls were settled in the sunny pantry with a litter of fluffy kittens to play with and a basket of washcloths and dish towels to fold.

The washroom was just off the kitchen, and with distance between them and the children and the chug-chug-chug of the wringer washer, Leah finally had the opportunity to question Anna about Wilmer's visit. Alone, it wasn't difficult to get the whole story from her sister.

"Wilmer admitted that he lost his temper and hit her," Anna said. "He knew he had done wrong, and he wants help to change. He asked Samuel to pray with him."

"And what did Samuel say?"

"You know my Samuel." Anna sighed and reached for a clean towel. "He is a good deacon—firm on church rules, but fair. It's not the first time he's admonished Wilmer for his bad treatment of Johanna. I know the Bible teaches us to forgive one another, but I worry for Johanna. Always, the same thing. Wilmer is sorry and he wants forgiveness."

"Only God can grant that kind of forgiveness," Leah answered, digging into the basket for a towel to fold. "And not unless we truly repent of what we have done wrong." She grimaced. "I'm afraid she'll go back to him. When he's sorry, he promises her that it won't happen again. And Johanna wants to believe that things will change…"

"Maybe you'd best go home and talk with her some more," Anna suggested. "I'll finish this folding. If you can just get those sheets through the wash, I can manage the rest here today."

"Are you sure?" Leah grabbed a sheet and began to feed it through the washer rollers, careful not to get her fingers too close to the mechanism.

"Johanna is more important than having my parlor floor scrubbed. We can do it together when you come back on Wednesday." Anna slid the heavy basket of clean wet laundry aside and gazed at her sister. "So, what is this I hear about you and the Mennonite missionary? Be careful, Leah. You know how people talk."

"Not you, too?"

"You rode to the Grange with him last night?" Anna rested her hands on her ample hips. "Lucky for you that he's going back to Africa soon."

"Africa?"

Anna shrugged. "Well, someplace foreign. I heard he was waiting to see where he'd be sent."

Leah didn't ask where Anna had heard that. The Amish didn't have telephones, but that didn't keep them from spreading every morsel of news from one end of the county to the other faster than the English could manage it on their fancy computers. *Amish telegram,* the English called it.

"I went with Daniel and Miriam and Charley and the Gleaners…and Rebecca and Susanna… to see the missionary program. He gave a bunch of us a ride in his aunt's van."

"And?" Anna waited.

"And after the program, Daniel asked me if I'd like to help out at the food bank in Dover tomorrow. Both of his cousins will be there. Caroline and Leslie Steiner. You know them. They buy eggs from us."

"And you are going to this Mennonite place?"

"Yes, I am. To help people in need. I told Mam I was, and she didn't tell me not to."

"Umm." Anna's expression was thoughtful. "Is he handsome, this Mennonite boy?"

"Nice-looking, yes, but…"

"You like him, don't you? You can tell me."

"There isn't anything to tell." Leah retrieved a stray sock that had dropped to the concrete floor and guided that through the washer rollers.

"Ah. That's what I told Samuel. You wouldn't do anything to cause a scandal. And not with a Mennonite."

"And if I did?"

"I would tell you to think over what you do… but I would love you all the same." Anna reached for her bag of wooden clothespins. "Help me hang out these sheets and then go on home. Johanna will listen to you if she'll listen to anyone."

"I think I should," Leah said. "I told Rebecca not to let her take one step out of the house, but Johanna…"

"It's hard to tell Johanna anything," Anna agreed. "But this time, I think we have to try."

Leah climbed the stile and hurried across the pasture. All the way home, she went over and over in her head what argument she would use to convince Johanna to stay at Mam's with the children. But when she met Susanna, who was on her way to the pigpen with a bucket of potato peelings and kitchen scraps, Leah's worse fears were realized.

"Johanna went home," Susanna said.

"Did Wilmer come to get her?"

"Ya." Susanna nodded. "In the buggy."

Leah sucked in a breath. "Rebecca was supposed to keep her here."

"Ya." Susanna's round face crinkled and her eyes grew large. "'Becka is sad."

"It's all right," Leah told her. "I'll go and talk to Johanna."

"Me, too."

"*Ne,* you stay here and help Rebecca and Aunt Jezzy. Tell them I'm going to take Dat's buggy and drive over to Johanna's. I should be home before Mam gets home from school."

"Okay." Susanna's brow furrowed.

"What is it, Susanna banana?" It was the name that always made her laugh.

"I'm thinking."

"What about?" Leah was anxious to get to Johanna's, but it was important to listen to Susanna. Just because she'd been born with Down syndrome—which made speech and some tasks difficult for her—didn't mean that Susanna was a child. She understood far more than most people realized.

Her little sister's chin firmed in an expression that looked exactly like their mother's. "Ruffie is married."

Leah nodded. "Yes, she is. To Eli."

"And Miriam is married to Charley."

Leah waited.

The tip of Susanna's tongue touched her upper lip. "And…and Anna…"

"Married Samuel," Leah finished.

"Can I marry Samuel, too?"

"No. Samuel is Anna's husband. You'd have to marry someone else."

"Who?" Susanna wrinkled her nose. "Not Irwin. I don't want to marry Irwin."

"Good. I'm glad you don't want to marry Irwin." Leah smiled at her to cover her sudden rush of sorrow. It was impossible to tell this precious sister that she'd never marry, never have a home and children of her own. "Because we can't have any more weddings now," she said, making a joke of it.

"Why not?"

"Because. Mam used up all her celery. You'll have to wait to get married, Susanna. Until you're older." Celery was traditionally served in large quantities at Amish weddings, and the joke was that you could tell who had a courting daughter by how many rows of celery a couple grew in their garden.

"Old as you?"

"Older than that," Leah said. "Twenty-five, at least. How old are you now?"

"Eighteen."

"Right. So that's years and years to be Mam's helper before you're old enough. Now, you go on and feed the pigs and then tell Rebecca where I went."

"To Johanna's house." Susanna picked up the bucket.

"That's right."

"Okay. Tell her to plant celery." Susanna giggled. "Maybe you want to get married. Next week!"

Leah drove Blackie and the courting buggy to Johanna and Wilmer's small farm at a fast trot. She didn't take pleasure in driving, as her sister Miriam did, but she was at ease around horses. She wasn't afraid to take them out on the road, and she was undaunted by cars and trucks. Once, when she'd been driving home with Anna and Rebecca from Spence's Auction, she'd heard the wail of fire engines coming toward them. She'd jumped out of the buggy, put her apron over the horse's eyes and led horse and carriage off onto the grass until the noisy vehicles had safely passed.

She hoped that once she reached Johanna's, she'd get a chance to be alone with her, but she doubted that she would. That was all right. She wasn't afraid of Wilmer. Church member or not, she'd tell him what she thought of him. For once, she wished that she had studied and taken her baptism when Anna did. Baptized women were treated as full adults, regardless of their age, and her word would have more sway in the community if she had joined the church. Surely, none of that would matter to Johanna. If they had a chance to talk this out, she'd be able to convince her sister that the only sensible course to take was to gather up Katy and Jonah and come home to Mam's to live.

Leah was still going over in her mind what argument she would use when she guided Blackie into Johanna's rutted dirt driveway. The small farmhouse had seen better days. The roof leaked and Leah suspected that the walls weren't insulated. Sometimes, in the winter, the children had to wear their coats while playing inside, and Katy got a lot of colds. Still, the rent was what they could afford, and the farm had a lot of outbuildings that Johanna was able to use for her poultry and sheep.

As she tied Blackie to the hitching rail, her sister stepped out on the porch. "Leah." Johanna's face was strained, but Leah couldn't see any new bruises. "Why are you here?"

"You know why." Leah started toward her.

Johanna came down the wobbly wooden steps and embraced her. "I know you mean well," she said, "but I have to work this out for myself."

"I'm afraid for you," Leah answered.

"Pray for me—pray for us."

"I have, and I still wish you'd come home with the children. Home to stay, at least for a few months."

Johanna shook her head. "I can't, Leah. Wilmer is my husband. He needs me—now, more than ever. He's not well."

"You won't be either, if you stay with him."

"We'll be all right. Really. Wilmer's been to talk to Samuel, and he plans to make a full confession in front of the church elders. He's sorry, and he's praying that nothing like that will ever happen again."

"And if it does?"

"I'll face that if I have to." She forced a smile. "But I don't want you and Mam to worry about me. Wilmer's sister, Emily, is coming to stay with us for a while. I like her. She's easy to get along with, and there won't be any trouble in the house while Emily is here."

"You're sure?" Leah stepped back and folded her arms. "I wish…"

"If wishes were horses…" Johanna said. It was an old saying of Dat's. *If wishes were horses, beggars would ride.*

They laughed together, and for an instant, Leah saw a flash of her old fun-loving and strong sister. "I love you," Leah said. She glanced toward the house.

"And I love you. But I know better than to let you and Wilmer under the same roof together until this whole thing blows over."

"What he did was wrong, Johanna. Don't make light of it."

"I'm not. Believe me, I'm not. But I have to accept that he can change—that God can show us a better way to live, in peace and harmony, for the sake of our children."

"I hope you're right," Leah said. She hugged Johanna again and then went back to where Blackie stood, patiently waiting.

"I see you're driving Dat's courting buggy," Johanna said. "Not planning on going riding with that Mennonite boy, are you?"

"Nooo." Leah chuckled and shook her head. "Mam had to tell you about Daniel, didn't she?"

"I'm your big sister. Just because I don't live in the house doesn't mean I can't know what's going on."

"And try to boss me around as you did when we were kids," Leah teased.

Johanna smiled. "Exactly. Sometimes, I wish we were still children. Everything seemed so easy then." Leah unsnapped Blackie's bridle and rolled the length of rope around the hitching rail. "Tell Mam I'll be fine. I'm sorry I worried all of you. With God's help, I can handle this."

As she drove out onto the blacktop road again, Leah wished that she could feel as confident as Johanna that she and her husband would be able to work out the problems in their marriage. She wished that she had Johanna's faith. It wasn't that she doubted that God could work miracles, but she'd always believed that God wanted her to take an active role in finding solutions.

Now, her thoughts wandered from Johanna's problems to her own. She had always believed that she would eventually find a good Amish boy, marry him and lead the same life as her mother and older sisters. It was what was expected of her—what every faithful young woman was supposed to do. And yet… She had always felt constrained by the rules, rules that Johanna, Ruth, Miriam, and Anna accepted without question. Now she wondered if what she'd been struggling with hadn't been her own willful disobedience, but something else. Could it be that God's plan for her was different than that of her sisters? And if it was, would she have the courage to heed His will and follow a new road into the unknown?

The consequences of such a departure from all she'd ever known—from everyone she'd ever loved—were frightening. Once, before she was too young to go to school, Mam and Dat had taken them to the ocean for a day of picnicking, fishing and playing on the beach. She and her sisters had been playing tag with the waves, running down the wet sand and letting the cold salt water wash over their feet and legs. But she had grown bold, dashing farther and farther into the surf, until suddenly the force of the water swept her off her feet.

She'd been tumbled over and over in the waves. She was terrified, as salt water burned her eyes and filled her nose and throat. She'd been certain that she was dying, but then, just as abruptly, her father's hand had closed around her waist. Dat had pulled her, choking and coughing out of the ocean, and the light was so bright that it nearly blinded her.

When she could see again—when she could make out her beloved father's face—she realized that she wasn't where she'd thought she was. She didn't see Mam or her sisters or the rock jetty. The undertow had carried her down the beach to a new spot, and her father had rescued her there. She'd always remembered that feeling and that exhilaration of being alive and safe…but in a new place.

Could that be what was happening to her now? Could meeting Daniel and stepping into his world be a repeat of her childhood experience of dashing into the waves? And if the undertow caught her again, would she be saved or lost? And if she survived, would she surface in a new and unknown life?

Blackie snorted and tossed his head, jerking Leah back to the present. Just ahead of her, on the side of the road, was a gray van. And getting out of the vehicle was a familiar figure, with soft brown hair.

Daniel…her Daniel.

Chapter Nine

Daniel slapped his palm on the van's steering wheel and groaned. How could he have forgotten the last thing his aunt had said to him before he left for the grocery store in her minivan? "Don't forget to put gas in the tank. Otherwise, you'll be walking home."

He *had* forgotten, and he *would* be walking. He'd tried to reach the house on his cell, but no one answered. He tried Leslie, but got her voice mail. *How could he have been so absentminded? Again!* He couldn't help but laugh.

He'd been so proud of himself for remembering to use Aunt Joyce's detergent coupons, getting everything on the list, including the twenty cans of tuna and the dozen boxes of raisins that he'd purchased with his own money. He hadn't wanted to show up at the food bank without his own donation.

Caroline would tease him unmercifully for forgetting to put gas in the van and getting stranded, and he had to admit that he deserved it. The truth was, he'd been thinking about Leah Yoder. He'd hardly been able to think of much else since the night they'd searched for Joey Beachy. He'd mentioned it to his aunt at breakfast this morning, and she'd rolled her eyes.

"What's wrong with Leah?" he'd asked, stung by the expression on her face.

"Nothing. Everything." Aunt Joyce had patted his shoulder as she slid his plate of eggs and grits in front of him. "She's a lovely girl…but…"

"She's Amish," Uncle Allan had finished.

Daniel had tried to make a joke of it. "Didn't you just say that Mom was hinting for you to introduce me to some nice girls while I was here?"

Aunt Joyce took her seat across from him and gave him an *I'm saying this for your own good* look. "She did. But what she meant was that I should introduce you to some nice *Mennonite* girls. Girls like Kelsie Rhinehart or Janelle Warner. Girls from our church."

"The Amish are a closed society," his uncle said as he buttered a slice of rye toast. "Leah Yoder's people have no interest in spreading the Gospel or in serving God by contributing to society. That's *our* way, Daniel. Leah's a beautiful girl, someone that I'd be proud to have as a daughter, but she's not a wise choice for you to show an interest in."

"What your uncle's trying to say," his aunt interjected, "is that we know these people. Fewer than 2 percent of the young women ever leave the church. Leah might date you, but if you have any other hopes, you're going to be sadly disappointed. None of Hannah Yoder's girls will ever leave the fold."

His uncle had folded his newspaper and set it aside. "And you're not just any Mennonite young man," he said. "You've had a calling to serve, and you're about to leave on another mission, probably to some place thousands of miles from home. You need to find a young woman who shares your faith and commitment."

"Someone like Kelsie," his aunt added. "I know she's interested. Her mother hopes you'll accept their invitation to dinner before you leave."

"You know how much we think of you," Uncle Allan said. "…And how proud we are of you. We just don't want to see you get hurt."

Daniel had tried to reassure them that he wasn't going to do anything stupid or anything to embarrass them, but he couldn't deny that he was interested in Leah…more than interested— fascinated. Yet, in all honesty, he wasn't ready to tell anyone how deeply he felt for Leah, especially since they were still practically strangers.

What his uncle had said was true. Every lesson Daniel had ever learned in his church and family had encouraged service to those less fortunate. Not every Mennonite felt called to serve as a missionary, but most who were active in the church helped to provide a safety net for those in need. They acted as volunteers in homeless shelters and youth programs, provided support for abused women and teen mothers. The Amish, while good, God-fearing people, kept to themselves. The sensible thing would be to find someone like Kelsie Rhinehart, someone who shared the same beliefs and sense of purpose.

But, Daniel thought as he got out of the van and locked the door, rational thinking had gone out the window when Leah walked into his life in that wet and windy dark pasture. Kelsie Rhinehart was a pleasant young woman, with a nice smile, but she wasn't Leah.

He'd only met Leah three times. It was ridiculous that he could be so attracted to her after knowing her for such a short time—laughable, really. Only he wasn't laughing. All he could think of was Leah…how she talked…the way she smiled…the sparkle in her eyes. He'd never met a girl like her—a girl who made him feel as though she lit up the room when she walked into it. And he'd never expected an Amish girl to be so outspoken or so easy to talk to. She was a puzzle, one he found fascinating.

He wanted to date Leah, but more than that, he wanted her to be his wife. It was insane. He'd never even had a steady girlfriend. He had lots of friends who were female, and he'd participated in coed youth outings, Sunday School picnics and organized sports. In Spain, he'd met lots of pretty girls and worked with them on festivals and charity affairs. He'd gone to movies and museums with a circle of friends from his high school, but he never felt comfortable asking a girl out.

He was probably getting way ahead of himself, anyway—he didn't even know if Leah liked him. She'd agreed to help out at the food bank, but that was probably because she had a kind heart. If she knew that he wanted to ask her out, she'd probably refuse to ever speak to him again. And her family would certainly shut the door to their home in his face.

Daniel grimaced. What was he thinking? There was absolutely no way that he has a chance with a girl like Leah Yoder, especially one as beautiful as she was. No, his hopes would come to nothing. He would end up as alone as he'd ever been in the girlfriend department, and

Leah would be the wife of a farmer like Samuel Mast—one of her own kind.

He walked a few yards from the van, and then turned back to make certain he'd locked the door. He hadn't seen any cars come by since he'd run out of gas and coasted off the road, but with all those groceries in the back, he didn't want to take chances. He took out his cell and tried his aunt's home again, but no one answered. As he retraced his steps, he couldn't help wondering how he'd gotten to this age without ever becoming seriously involved with a girl, any girl.

He supposed that part of it was that he'd always looked younger than he was. At eighteen, he could have passed for a middle school student, and he'd been nearly twenty before he'd shot up another four inches and begun to shave. The girls he talked to at lunch and between classes all treated him like a younger brother and wanted to tell him their problems with their boyfriends.

In college, he'd been so engrossed in his nursing studies and the multiple part-time jobs that he'd worked to support himself—that there hadn't been time for dating. And even though he was lonely, at times, the girls in the too-tight clothing with flirtatious personalities didn't seem like a good fit for him, and the more studious ones, who did interest him, he'd been too shy to approach.

Daniel considered himself a normal guy, but he'd never been able to understand the games that a lot of young men and women played or the way they flirted with each other. He wasn't interested in parties, where the main attraction seemed to be alcohol, and he didn't want to hang out in bars, hoping to meet some girl who'd go home with him. As geeky as it sounded, even to himself, he'd wanted to save some important parts of life for the one woman he was certain God intended for him.

For Daniel, marriage was a sacred pact between one man and one woman. He'd always felt that the greatest gifts he could bring to that union was a pure heart, a sense of responsibility and a strong faith. He'd thought that when the right girl came along, the one God intended for him, he'd know it. He just hadn't expected that girl to appear in an Amish *kapp* with a good flashlight and a better sense of direction than he'd ever possess.

Daniel glanced down the road. He hoped that the nearest gas station would have a sympathetic attendant willing to lend him a gas can and perhaps offer a ride back to the van. He had money. He even had a credit card that his church had secured for him so that he wouldn't travel on this speaking tour without an emergency backup. But he hadn't used church money for gasoline or tolls, at least not so far. He'd saved most of the small salary he'd collected while working at the clinic in Spain, and he'd been using that for his day-to-day needs.

The rattle of wheels on the blacktop behind him and the clack-clack-clack of a horse's hooves pulled Daniel out of his reflection. He stopped walking and turned to see an open buggy approaching. There was one person inside, a woman in a dark green dress and a white head covering. For an instant, he thought it might be…

But then he laughed and waved at the driver. What was he thinking? Just because he had Leah Yoder on his brain didn't mean that she could materialize out of thin air just when he needed a ride.

The woman waved back, and as she came closer, excitement rose in Daniel's chest. It couldn't be…but the driver was young and pretty, and she was…

"Daniel? Did your aunt's van break down?"

Daniel stared. "Leah?"

She laughed. "*Ne,* it's Bishop Atlee." She reined up the horse. "Of course it's me." She paused. "Well, are you getting in, or are you going to keep walking?"

"You're here." He still couldn't believe it. It was Leah. *His* Leah. "What are you doing here—on this road?"

The horse tossed its head and pawed at the road with one iron-shod hoof. "Hurry up," Leah urged. "Get in before he starts acting up."

"In the buggy?"

She laughed again. "Did you fall and hit your head, Daniel Brown? Of course, in the buggy. Are you on your way home? I'm afraid I don't have any tools in the back for fixing car engines." Her eyes sparkled with mischief. "And if I did, I wouldn't know the first thing about repairing one."

"Yes, all right." He moved cautiously up to the buggy. "How do I…"

She chuckled. "Just climb in."

The horse shifted from side to side and switched his tail as Daniel scrambled up onto the seat beside Leah. He'd no sooner gotten his balance than she clicked to the animal and the buggy started forward with a jolt. Daniel grabbed for the front panel. "I've never ridden in one of these before," he admitted.

"I can see that." She flicked the long leather lines and the black horse began to trot. A truck came down the road toward them, and Leah tightened her grip on the reins but didn't slow the horse.

"I ran out of gas," Daniel explained. "I was walking to a gas station."

"Does it happen a lot?"

"Does what happen?" He tried not to stare at her, but she was so pretty with her red hair and the modest dark green dress.

"Running out of gas," she said. "Do you do it a lot?"

"More than I should." He laughed with her. "You've probably guessed. I'm a little absent-minded. I get so engrossed in what I'm doing or what I'm thinking about that I forget to do stuff. I lay down my keys and can't remember where I put them. I misplace my textbooks or—"

"Forget it's time to go to work?" she suggested.

"No." He grinned at her. "My work is the only place I don't forget things. I'm on time, and I know what I'm doing." His voice grew earnest. "I'm a good nurse, Leah. I might not pay attention to what time I'm supposed to leave at the end of the day and work a double shift, but—"

"Then you have nothing to be ashamed of," Leah put in. "I probably wouldn't think to put gas in an automobile, either."

"No, you wouldn't forget." He grimaced. "You don't forget to feed this horse, and you wouldn't forget what a van needs to run. I don't see you as a distracted person. You have purpose."

"You think so? I wonder." She made a soft clicking noise to the horse and guided it off the road as a large brown delivery truck passed them. "Mam says that everyone is born with strengths and weaknesses. We have to do our best with what God gave us. It seems to me that you do just fine." She chuckled. "For an Englisher."

"I'm not an Englisher," he protested. "I'm Mennonite."

She shrugged. "Same as. You aren't *Plain*. You've lived in foreign cities and flown in airplanes."

"Guilty." He smiled at her, thinking that talking to Leah was the most natural thing he'd ever done. "If you could take me to a gas station, that would be great," he said. "I can probably get a ride back to the van from—"

"I'll just take you back to the van," she interrupted. "Unless you're afraid people will laugh at you, riding in an Amish buggy."

"No, that doesn't bother me. I like being with you."

She nodded. "Me, too, Daniel."

"I like the way you say my name."

She chuckled. "So it's settled. I'll bring you back to your van. Do you think it will start?"

"Oh, sure. It's a reliable vehicle. It wasn't completely empty. It started sputtering, and I knew instantly what I'd done wrong. I turned the key off and steered it onto the grass."

"Smart."

Daniel laughed. "Trying to fix what I'd already messed up. I would have had my truck, but my uncle borrowed it this morning to bring home some lumber. We're going to repair the back porch." He shrugged. "He's the carpenter. I'm the run-and-fetch guy."

"Someone has to run and fetch, with any job."

He glanced down at her slender hands, so small and yet strong enough to control the big horse. "I've never driven a horse and carriage," he said.

"Would you like to learn?"

"You mean now?"

Her eyes twinkled with amusement. "Well, there is a horse available right now."

He hesitated, feeling totally out of his element, but wanting to try. "I warn you, I'm not familiar with horses."

She smiled at him, and he felt as though the oxygen had suddenly disappeared from the air. *She's the one,* he thought. *Bonnet or no bonnet. If I mess this up, I'll regret it for the rest of my life.* "You look so pretty today," he managed. "So confident, holding those reins."

"I don't look so good, I think." She smoothed down her skirt. "It's my day to help out my sister, Anna. We were doing the wash. I think I got more water on me than on the clothes." She passed the reins to him and a thrill ran up his arms as her hands brushed against him. "Hold them like this," she instructed. "Firm, but not too tight. A horse's mouth is sensitive."

"His mouth?"

"The lines lead to the bridle, and the bridle has a bit that fits into his mouth. Without the bridle, it would be hard to control such a large animal."

"He's big, all right." Daniel tried not to show how nervous he was.

"Big, but not as smart as a pig or a dog. Horses frighten easily. You have to let them know that you're the boss."

"Even when I don't *feel* like I'm the boss?"

"Exactly." She nodded in approval. "Good. You have good hands, Daniel, gentle hands. Not clumsy."

The horse continued to move along the blacktop, almost as if it didn't know he was holding the reins instead of Leah. Daniel's mouth was dry, but he was having a good time. He tried to think of something sensible to say, so that Leah wouldn't think he was a total dork. "Anna's married to Samuel, isn't she?" was the best he could come up with.

Leah nodded. "They're newlyweds. Samuel was a widower with five children. Anna is a good housekeeper, and she'll make a good mother, but it takes a while to get into a routine. I go over a few days every week to do what I can."

"That's good of you. You get along well with your sister, then?" Another vehicle came up behind them and honked the horn. The horse raised its head and made a little jump to the left. Daniel tensed up and tightened his hands on the reins.

"Easy, boy," Leah said to the horse. She laid a hand over his and he felt the same jolt of excitement. "Don't wrap the line around your fist," she said. "That could be dangerous. You're doing fine. Keep the lines gripped so."

He did as she instructed. "Like this?"

"Yes, very good. A few more lessons and you'll be fit to go." She settled back onto the bench seat as the driver raced around the buggy and continued on down the road. "Everyone gets along with Anna," she said, answering his question. "...Even my *Grossmama.*" Leah wrinkled her nose. "My grandmother. You met her. She is a strong..." She searched for a word.

"Personality?"

They laughed together. "*Grossmama* doesn't like my mother so much, but she likes Anna. They get along fine. Anna and Samuel have asked her to come and live with them, so it will make life easier for Mam, too. But that won't happen 'til later, Anna and Samuel being newlyweds and all. They need their time alone together." She felt her cheeks grow warm, with the embarrassment of such talk, but Daniel didn't seem to notice.

"Where were you going now? Am I taking you out of your way?" he asked. "I'm sorry if—"

"No." Leah shook her head. "Just on my way home. My sister, Johanna…" She hesitated and then went on in a softer voice. "Her husband is not well, not sick but…troubled. I worry about Johanna and her children."

"You were on your way to her house?" Daniel straightened his spine. Driving the horse was easier than he'd thought, at least with Leah beside him. She was a good teacher.

"On my way back home from Johanna's." She turned her face away, seemingly staring at the horse's rump. For a long moment, she didn't speak, and then she sighed. "I shouldn't say anything, especially to an outsider, but I feel like you're not the kind of man to judge." She hesitated. "Wilmer, that's Johanna's husband, he does things to her."

Daniel took his gaze off the road ahead and glanced at Leah. "What kind of things?"

"He gets angry and shouts at her. A lot. And he hit her. She had a bruise on her cheek." Leah touched her cheekbone. "Here. An ugly bruise."

"No man should ever hit a woman. Ever."

"I agree. I wanted Johanna to bring the children home and stay with us. But it's not easy. We…the Amish don't believe in breaking up families. A marriage is for life."

"With us, too," Daniel agreed. "But not if there's abuse. That's against the law."

Leah reached over his hands, gripped the reins and pulled back. The horse stopped short. "I shouldn't have said anything to you. My sister… my family would be angry with me. It's private, what happens in our homes."

"But hitting a woman—hitting anyone is wrong."

"Yes, it is."

"Your mother must…" He broke off, not sure what her mother thought about such behavior. "I mean, surely, she…"

"My mother is worried, but she says that Johanna must make her own decision, that we can't make it for her. And Johanna is still trying to mend things between her and Wilmer."

"And you're afraid your sister is in danger."

"Exactly."

"And you say there are children?"

"A four-year-old boy and a baby girl. Johanna says he won't harm the children. I think Wilmer is too hard on Jonah. He favors their daughter. He has since she was born. Wilmer says he's sorry for what he did to Johanna, and I know we should forgive, but—"

"If it were my sister, I don't know if I could forgive a man for striking her."

Moisture glistened on Leah's lashes. "You understand how I feel."

He nodded. "Maybe you should report this to the police."

"No, I can't. Not yet. My sister would never forgive me. We try to fix things inside our church…in our community. But Johanna will be safe now, at least for a while. Wilmer's sister is coming to stay with them. He wouldn't lose his temper in front of her." Leah released the leather lines and clicked to the animal. "Walk on, Blackie." She rested her hand on his forearm. "Promise me that you won't tell anyone."

The horse obeyed her command and the buggy moved forward. "Not if you don't want me to," Daniel said.

"Please," she pleaded. "It was wrong of me to talk about my sister's marriage, but I had to talk to someone…someone outside the family."

"I won't break your confidence."

"Oh, no!" Leah pulled her hand from his.

Daniel glanced up to see another horse and buggy, a larger, covered, black carriage coming toward them. "What's wrong?" he asked.

Leah grimaced. "That's my Aunt Martha."

"Is that a problem?"

"I'm afraid so, Daniel. My Aunt Martha is always a problem."

Chapter Ten

Leah's heart sank as she smiled and waved. Of all the people she knew, it would have to be Martha and Dorcas who saw her with Daniel. "I wonder where they're going," she said, trying to keep her voice light.

Dorcas stared but waved back, while Aunt Martha only gave a grudging nod as the buggies passed each other.

"Will you be in trouble because of me?" Daniel asked.

Leah hesitated. *How could she make him understand Aunt Martha without being uncharitable?* "It's not your fault," she said. "Don't worry about it. You've done nothing wrong. What would be wrong would be for me to leave a friend walking, instead of picking him up."

"So…are we friends?"

Her heart skipped a beat. "Yes, Daniel, I think

we are. Since the woods and the dark…" She glanced at him and smiled. "And the rain." She nodded. "Yes, I'm sure of it—friends."

"It was a miserable night for a walk in the woods—but we found Joey."

"Yes, we did. We found him together." Daniel grinned at her, and Leah found herself drawn into the depths of his warm green eyes.

"You found Joey. I just tagged along."

"Is that what you think?" She shook her head. "No, *we* did it. If it wasn't for you, I wouldn't have been so brave. I don't like the dark. My sisters always tease me about being afraid to go out to the barn at night. It's why I always have a flashlight." She reached under the seat and showed him the one she kept in this buggy. "And I wouldn't have been able to save that baby goat."

"You don't know that."

"You're too hard on yourself, Daniel."

"Maybe, sometimes." He swallowed and his gaze became serious. "You're different than most girls, Leah. Easy to talk to. I feel like I've known you forever."

She smiled. "Me too, with you, I mean."

"Okay, one friend to another—why is my being in this buggy with you a problem?"

"It's my aunt. She's…" There was nothing to

do but be honest with Daniel. "My aunt is something of a *retschbeddi*."

He chuckled. "A tattletale?"

She covered her face with her hands. "You know more *Deutsch* than you let on."

"A little, but my accent is awful."

"It's what I think about my English. In the home we speak German a lot...and with other Amish. My mother wanted us to use good English out in the world."

"I like your mother," he murmured.

"I've been blessed to have her...and my father. Both good people."

"And your Aunt Martha? Is she your mother's sister?"

Leah shook her head. "My Dat was her only brother. She was older. He said she tried to always boss him when they were growing up. My *Grossmama*—you met her at our house— she is their mother. Aunt Martha takes after her, I think. My aunt watches what my sisters and I do, and she tells whoever will listen."

He chuckled. "She's judgmental?"

"Exactly." Leah sighed. "My sister, Miriam, thinks Aunt Martha has a grudge against my mother. It's true Aunt Martha never cared much for Mam, but I don't believe she intends harm. Beneath her stern outside is a tender heart. I have to think Aunt Martha means well and is trying to guide us to live a *Plain* life."

"So, in her eyes, us riding together is wrong."

Leah nodded. "She definitely won't approve, especially since we're riding in this buggy, and you're driving." She flashed him a mischievous smile. "Aunt Martha will make a lot more of it than it is."

"Why *this* buggy?"

"Because it isn't closed. Anyone can see us—see what we're doing. It's called a courting buggy. If you were Amish, and I was with you, people would think we were *walking out* together."

"By *walking out,* you mean dating?"

"Dating, yes, but a little more serious than that. If we were coming home from a young people's frolic—a singing or a picnic—that would be one thing. But we're together in the middle of the day, not part of a group, so other Amish would see us as getting serious about one another."

"And they wouldn't if we were together in a closed buggy?"

"If I'd been driving Mam's closed buggy, I would have picked you up, but I would have worried some. I might even have offered to find you help or go for the gas, but not asked you to ride with me."

"I'm not sure I understand the logic."

She chuckled again. "It's logical to me, but I'm Amish. I wouldn't expect you to understand."

"Pretend I was Amish. Would I be suitable to ride with you—in your Aunt Martha's eyes?" The buggy bumped over a rough spot in the road. "Do you want to take the reins? Am I driving all right?"

"You're doing fine."

He glanced at the front left wheel. "That looks a little wobbly. The whole carriage seems small and light. Are you sure it's safe to drive on this road?"

"It's a solid buggy," she assured him. "My Dat brought it with him from his home in Pennsylvania. He courted my mother in this buggy, and he always kept it in great shape."

They reached the intersection of a busier road. "I'll take over now," she said. "Blackie gets a little skittish when the big trucks pass." He handed over the reins and Leah guided the animal onto the blacktop and then onto the right shoulder. A car whizzed by them without slowing down. The horse flinched but kept trotting.

"If you were Amish, hmm." Leah took a moment to consider his question. "First," she said, "it might depend if you were from our church or one equally conservative. We're very strict, compared to some communities. You see?" She pointed to the waistband on her dress. "No buttons. Our women use straight pins. In some churches, men are allowed to use buttons, but they must be small and not fancy. It's because back in the old countries, in Germany and Switzerland, before we came to America, soldiers wore shiny buttons on their uniforms. We were driven from our homes, tortured and sometimes burned at the stake by soldiers because of our religion."

He nodded. "I know the history of the persecutions. It was the same with the Mennonites. You know that the Amish, your Amish, were once members of the Mennonite church?"

"Of course. Jacob Amman broke away from the Swiss Mennonites because he felt that they weren't strict enough. But we Amish still share many of the same customs with your church, such as foot washing after communion and believing in adult-only baptisms."

"Okay." Daniel ran a hand through his short hair. "Say that I am from your Amish church or one just as conservative. Then what would I have to do to satisfy your Aunt Martha?"

Leah turned her attention to a tractor-trailer coming down the road toward them. "Easy, boy," she cooed to Blackie. "Steady." And then to Daniel, she said, "It might depend on how well prepared you were to provide for a family. Are you a serious boy or one who has paid attention to lots of girls? Do you have a good trade? If you're a farmer, do you own land or have hope of inheriting some?"

"So, if I'm poor, I don't have a chance with you?"

"It depends. Do you own a good horse and buggy? Are you willing to work hard to learn new skills? How respectable is your family? Would your bishop or church elders speak for your character?"

"Sounds like your aunt is hard to please."

"She would be right to take all those things into consideration. Marriage is more than just between a man and a woman," Leah said. "It's of great importance to the family and the community. It's not a decision to take lightly."

"I agree," Daniel said. "But what if I didn't own land and didn't have a bishop to recommend me, but we really liked each other. Would you let me ride with you, then?"

Her pulse quickened. "I might," she answered softly. "I *am* riding with you. Tomorrow? The food bank? Will you and Caroline pick me up at the house?"

"Yes, about twelve-thirty, if that's all right."

For the next quarter of an hour, Leah steered the conversation to safer topics: what her duties would be as a volunteer and how many clients they could expect to serve. As they approached a quieter side street, she guided the horse left past several new houses with well-kept front yards. "There's a small convenience store at the next corner. They sell gas, and I'm sure they'll let you borrow a gas can."

"I'm glad you came along when you did and took pity on me," Daniel teased. "It would have been a long walk."

She laughed, then smiled shyly. "I want to thank you for listening…about Johanna."

"I know you're worried about her. I would be too. I wish I could do something to help."

"You have," she said sincerely. "Sometimes just talking to someone makes you feel better… But you won't say anything to anyone else, right?"

"Absolutely not, not unless you want me to. You can count on me, Leah."

A few minutes later, they reached the store with its two gas pumps outside. Daniel bought her a bottle of iced tea, and while she was waiting, a pickup pulled into the lot with Roland Byler sitting in the truck bed. By the time Daniel got his gas, Leah had invited Roland to ride home with them.

Leah quickly made the introductions. "Roland is Charley's brother. His usual ride was sick today and his boss drove out from the job site to pick him up. It will be a tight squeeze, but we can all fit, and it will save Roland's boss from driving him home."

Having Roland in the buggy kept her and Daniel from continuing their discussions about Johanna and Aunt Martha. Luckily, the two men seemed to hit it off, and by the time they got back to Daniel's van, the three of them were all laughing and joking as if they'd been long time friends.

"Thanks for the ride," Daniel said, once he got the big van's engine running. "See you tomorrow."

"Twelve-thirty," Leah replied.

As they drove away, she asked Roland how his wife was doing. A few weeks earlier, Pauline had suffered a miscarriage of twins. Due to juvenile diabetes, her health was unstable, and the pregnancy had been very stressful on her body. The community had rallied around the young family, helping out by bringing meals and taking care of two-year-old Jared so that Pauline could regain her strength. The medical bills were high, and Roland had taken a construction job for a few weeks to take up some of the slack.

"Better, by the grace of God," Roland answered as she passed the reins to him so that he could drive. "So many praying for her had to help. But she mourns the two she lost."

"That's natural," Leah said. "There can be nothing worse than the loss of a child for a mother."

"I hate to see Pauline grieving. But if I'd lost her, I don't know how I would have stood it. We've had so many close calls over the last few years. Having Jared is our miracle."

"A fine little boy he is, too. A blessing to you both."

Roland flicked the reins and Blackie crossed the intersection at a trot. "We were afraid he might be born with Pauline's sugar, but he wasn't. Not yet, at least. She worries over him day and night. Too much, I think." He sighed deeply. "It's good of the neighbors to watch him for her, and we appreciate it, but she's so afraid something will happen to him when he's away from her that I wonder if it's worth it."

Leah wasn't sure what to say. Miriam had mentioned the same thing to Mam, and she wasn't the only one. Other women in the congregation, including Aunt Martha, had noticed how obsessed Pauline had become with her son's health since she'd lost the babies. However, Leah didn't feel it was her place to add weight to Roland's burden.

But he didn't seem to notice that she hadn't spoken and continued on. "Don't get me wrong, Leah. I understand how much Pauline must be hurting, but Jared's not sick. He's strong, and it's not good for him to be shut up in the house with her so much. She doesn't trust me to take him in the buggy to church services or even to the barn anymore, for fear the cow will kick him or he'll climb the hayloft ladder and fall."

"We'll keep praying for her—for all three of you," Leah said. "And if there's anything we can do to help, just ask. Anything."

"Your family's been good to us—all of you. I can't thank you enough."

A van full of Amish men, driven by an English woman, passed. The men waved, and Leah and Roland waved back. "People will be saying we're courting, us being in your Dat's courting buggy."

It was good to see him smiling. Everyone in Seven Poplars liked Roland, and his name had been mentioned as a possible candidate for preacher the next time there was an opening. But, according to Charley, Pauline's illness had been hard on Roland. Usually a jolly and good-natured person, he'd become much more serious and quiet.

"Ya," she teased. "Maybe they'll say you're turning to one of those religions where you can have two wives at one time."

"Lord forbid! One wife is all I can manage. God gave me a good one, and I'll not tempt fate by looking elsewhere, not for love nor money." They came to Roland and Pauline's lane and he brought Blackie to a stop. "This is fine," he said. "I can walk up the drive." He swung down and got his tools out of the back. "But I'm curious. Is there something going on between you and that Mennonite, Daniel?"

"He's a friend. I found him with his van broke down. Was I to just drive by and leave him?"

Roland raised a brow suspiciously. "There's bound to be talk, and not about me. You be careful, Leah. A good reputation is the finest thing a woman can own. You wouldn't want to give people reason to think you'd stray from the path. Especially since your mother was born Mennonite."

"I'll keep that in mind, Roland," she answered, trying to keep from showing how the question peeved her. "After all, you know I'm at the running-around time." She lifted her brows. "No telling what I'll get up to."

"Amen to that." He grinned. "So long as you come to the church, be baptized and put on the black. We all think too much of you and your family to have it any other way."

"It's a matter of choice," she reminded him.

"It's a matter of your soul." He slung his tools over his back, turned, and strode up the lane. "Thanks for the ride," he called. "I appreciate it."

* * *

The next afternoon, Leah joined Daniel and
Caroline at the food bank. Leslie was supposed to help as well, but she'd lost a filling and
had to go to the dentist. That left the three of
them to unload food donations, keep the boxes
filled and wait on clients. Not only were they
on their feet from the moment they'd walked
into the building, but they barely had time to
catch their breath.

Leah was busy dealing with all sorts of people,
including several women who spoke only Spanish, an elderly man in a wheelchair with a hearing problem and a young mother with three
small, shrieking children.

At first Leah filled cardboard boxes with rice,
beans, canned fruit, powdered milk, pasta, jars
of spaghetti sauce and an assortment of canned
vegetables, while Daniel carried perishable
goods in from a refrigerated truck and moved
cases of food to the assembly tables. But soon
Caroline had a line of waiting and sometimes
impatient customers. Leah came to the front to
assist her, and when the crowd thinned out to just
a steady stream, Caroline traded jobs with her.
Leah had rarely spoken to so many Englishers
in one day, and she'd rarely had to deal with so
many questions and different situations.

The problem for her wasn't that she was overwhelmed by the task; rather it was that she had such a good time meeting new challenges. Most of the strangers she met were surprised to be waited on by an Amish woman, and the majority of them had questions about her clothing and her faith. She answered as simply and as clearly as possible while managing to retain her good humor. Many of the clients were facing hard times financially, and it was so rewarding to be able to help, if only in a small way.

Truly, Leah thought, she was getting more from volunteering than those who'd come to accept the donations. Ever since she could remember, her mother had kept in mind those in the community who were less fortunate. Leah and her sisters had helped prepare meals, can food to share with the elderly and the sick, and welcomed guests to their table at mealtime. But in her home, charity had always been offered within the Amish circle.

Mam had warned her that being among the English might tempt her to question her faith, but Leah was learning that it might not be in the way her mother thought it would be. Simply by taking part in assisting strangers who were having a difficult time feeding their children made Leah wonder why her church didn't extend a hand to outsiders. She'd always been taught that her people were God's chosen ones, that if they lived according to His word as revealed in the Bible and followed the rules of the *Ordnung*, they were living a good and proper life. But was it possible that God wanted something more from her? And had he meant for Daniel to cross her path and throw open a window to a larger world?

Leah was pondering that question when she realized that Daniel was speaking to her. She blinked, looked around and saw that Caroline was locking the front door and lowering the blinds.

"Leah? Did you hear me?"

"Yes...no." She chuckled. "Sorry, I was caught up in my own thoughts. Gathering hay in the mist, Mam would call it." She looked at Caroline. "Is it quitting time?"

"Past time," Caroline said. "We stayed open an extra twenty minutes. There's another shift coming later. The food bank is open three hours this evening, for people who work a day shift and can't get here in the afternoon, but we're done."

"I never expected so many to come," Leah said. She looked up into Daniel's expectant face. "Sorry, I didn't hear a word you said to me."

"He wants to know if you'll come to our house, this evening," Caroline said, removing her apron and hanging it on a hook. "We're filling shoeboxes for Daniel's orphanage."

"Not *my* orphanage," he said, "but one I vol-

unteered at when we lived in Marrakesh, in
Morocco. It was a haven for homeless boys who
live on the street. Caroline and Leslie organized
a drive to collect toothbrushes, toothpaste, pencils, toys and other small items that boys might
like. Some of them have never had anything new
that belonged to them personally—at least nothing that they didn't steal."

"Some of our friends are coming over," Caroline said. "Teenagers and young adults. Afterwards, Mom always has a movie party for us in
the basement. Popcorn and DVDs."

"Movies?" Leah asked. "What kind of movies?"
She loved movies and she'd been to them several
times with Mennonite friends when she was in
Ohio. But she didn't want to see anything with
violence or foul language. It simply wasn't something she thought she would enjoy.

"Usually Disney," Caroline assured her.
"Nothing that would upset our pastor or my
friends' parents. Mom would love for you to
come. She told us to be sure to invite you."

Leah hesitated. A movie and popcorn sounded
good, but what would Mam think? "Could I
bring Susanna?" she asked suddenly. "She would
love to see a movie."

"Of course," Caroline said. "Bring all your sisters if you like."

"All right," Leah said, nodding. "Thank you.

I will come." She smiled at Daniel. "And thank you for asking me."

"I'm glad you're coming," he said as his cousin walked away, "but that wasn't what I asked you."

Her eyes widened.

He took a deep breath and stepped closer. "I wanted to know…" He swallowed. "I wanted to know if you would go out with me."

Leah didn't know what to say. "You mean… like a date?"

He nodded. "Yes, a date. More than one. I want to get to know you, Leah. I'm asking if you'll walk out with me."

Chapter Eleven

"Can I think about it?"

That was the answer she'd given Daniel when he'd asked her if she'd date him. And she *had* been thinking about it. For hours and hours. She kept going over and over in her mind whether it was the right thing to do and what it might mean if she said *yes*. She'd prayed for God to tell her what she should do, but so far, He hadn't answered. Either that…or she hadn't listened hard enough.

Leah knew what she *wanted* to do. She wanted to accept, to go out with Daniel, to get to know him and his family. But was that rebellion against the rules that she felt were too strict? Did she want to be with Daniel because she was attracted to him, or was she attracted to the bigger world that Daniel represented? Was it Daniel's stories of the colorful Moroccan *souk*, the marketplace with snake charmers, acrobats and camels, that fascinated her? Or was it Daniel himself? How could she know what her heart was telling her and what was earthly temptation?

And if she did date Daniel and they liked each other, how would she explain that to her mother? She'd only known Daniel since Saturday. Surely, going against everything she'd ever believed for someone she'd just met was foolhardy, not worthy of one of Hannah Yoder's daughters.

Leah continued to wrestle with her conscience as she and Susanna helped fill the colorfully decorated boxes in the Steiners' basement. As she'd suspected, Susanna was thrilled at the idea of a movie and popcorn party. Everyone had been kind and welcoming to her sister, and Daniel had given her the special job of putting six pencils in every box.

"After pencils, I'm going to do cow…cow… cowalators!" Susanna said excitedly. "Daniel said I could."

"Calculators," Leah corrected softly.

Daniel smiled and winked at her, and she smiled back at him. After he and Caroline and Leslie had picked them up at the house, they'd made a quick stop at the dollar store. Daniel had purchased several dozen solar calculators, bags of marbles, index cards and other personal items for the boxes. Leah didn't need to buy anything to contribute. Mam had produced bags of erasers, packs of sticky notes, rulers and small pencil sharpeners shaped like basketballs to add to the donations, which Daniel said would be perfect.

"I still don't know how your mother could pull all these things out of a hat on such short notice," Leslie said. She and another friend, Gail, were rolling T-shirts and securing them with thick rubber bands.

"Not out of her bonnet," Susanna corrected proudly. "Out of her school chest."

Leah smiled. "Mam has a teacher's savings card for the big office supply store in Dover. In the fall, they have wonderful specials for back-to-school items, and she always comes home with baskets full of stuff for our kids."

Daniel laughed and shook his head. "I can just picture your mother driving up to the store in her buggy and loading her cart."

"We watch our budget like anyone else," Leah explained. "And if there's a bargain for good stuff, we're going to take advantage of it, just like everyone else. Amish are allowed in Staples, you know."

"Owwll." Daniel clutched his heart. "Stung again." Everyone laughed and he laughed with them. "Every time I open my mouth, I say something stupid."

"You're not stupid," Susanna said, pausing

in her careful counting of pencils. "Nobody is stupid. Just sometimes slow."

"But slow is good," Daniel's Aunt Joyce said as she approached the table with a pitcher of lemonade and homemade ginger cookies. "If you go slow, you don't miss anything good in life." She smiled as she looked at the rows of boxes. "This is wonderful. I didn't know how you'd manage to get all these donations in, but somebody here is organized."

"Leah!" Daniel, Leslie and Gail all said in unison.

"She thought of rolling the T-shirts instead of folding them, and they fit perfectly around the rulers," Caroline explained. "And when the box is full, we stuff the small stuff in the corners and tape it shut."

"I know the children will appreciate all your work," Joyce said.

"They will," Daniel agreed. "Some of the kids have never had a new T-shirt or school supplies that weren't worn or broken. But they don't whine about what they don't have. Most are grateful to have a safe place to sleep and enough food to eat." He exhaled softly. "I wish you could see these boys and look into their eyes. Even the little ones seem far older than their years. Anything we can do to help them is greatly appreciated."

Leah wished she could have been there with

Daniel to see the orphanage and meet the children who needed so much. Again, she was thankful to be of some assistance, however small. She was glad Mam had agreed to allow them to come this evening, even if *Grossmama* had put up a fuss. Of course, Mam wouldn't have forbidden her to go, but she could have kept her from bringing Susanna if she'd truly believed the evening was inappropriate. "Leah?"

Daniel was standing at her side. "I'm on popcorn detail. It seems *someone*—" He gave Caroline an amused look and everyone laughed. "Someone we all know and love has decimated the popcorn supply and I've been designated to run out and buy more. Would you ride with me while the rest finish taping up the boxes?"

Leah glanced at Susanna.

"She'll be fine," Daniel's aunt said. "She can help me pick out a movie. What do you think, Susanna?" she asked. "*Swiss Family Robinson, Old Yeller,* or *The Yearling?*"

"All of them!" Susanna cried.

Leah nodded. "I'll go with you, Daniel." She followed him up the narrow basement steps, through the kitchen and outside to where his truck was parked. He opened the door for her and she climbed in.

"So," he asked as he got behind the wheel. "Is tonight a date?"

"No." She smiled at him. "This is not a date. We're helping the homeless children. It's a service frolic."

"And working in the food bank today—was that a date?"

She shook her head. "Definitely not."

"Hmm." He turned the key and put the truck into gear. "You're not going to make this easy for me, are you?"

She didn't answer.

"But would you go out with me…on a *date* date?"

"I told you, I'll think about it." She straightened her *kapp*. She'd thought that she and Susanna might feel out of place here tonight in their Amish dress, but Caroline's friends all wore prayer caps, some small and lacy, yet all had head coverings. Their clothing wasn't *Plain*, but it wasn't fancy, either. Caroline's skirt and blouse were homemade, simple and modest, nearly identical to those of her mother and sister except in color. Daniel and the two other young men who'd come to help wore blue jeans and white button-up shirts.

If Daniel had some misconceptions about the Amish, she had her own about the Mennonites. Far from ungodly people, Daniel's relatives and friends seemed to put God first in their work and play. The Mennonite young people seemed open about their faith and willing to share God's word with others. It wasn't what she'd expected.

"I like you a lot, Leah," Daniel said, tugging her back into the moment. He eased the truck out onto the country road. "I think you like me, too."

"I do," she admitted in a small voice. "But I'm afraid."

"I'd never do anything to hurt you." He reached over and took her hand. "You have to believe that, Leah."

She let her hand lie in his for just a few seconds before withdrawing it. "That's the problem. If we walk out together…if we find out that we aren't a good match, then that would almost be better. But what if we found that we liked each other even more?" She sighed. How could she explain how she felt to Daniel? "We've only just met. This is all too fast for me."

He slowed the truck, put on his signal and pulled over along the side of the road. "I know it's happening quickly," he said. "But every good change I've made in my life has been a spur-of-the-moment decision. I think I knew that you were the one that very first time we met." He took a deep breath. "I've prayed over this, Leah, and I think God brought us together. I may not have much time in Delaware before I get my new assignment. I don't want to waste a single moment."

"I've prayed over it, too," she said. Her heart was racing, and she could still feel a warm tingling in the palm of her hand from where he'd touched her. "But God hasn't answered. I don't know what He wants me to do."

"All the more reason we should date, so that we can make a rational decision."

"Dating you would mean going against my family, my community."

He met her eyes. "My aunt and uncle aren't too happy about it, either, probably for the same reasons."

"If we…if we got serious, it would mean…"

"We'd marry," he finished for her. "I think that's what I want. I think I love you."

She turned to look at him, a little shocked by his forwardness, but at the same time…fascinated by how sure he was of himself. "How can you love me? How can I love you? We don't know each other." Now she was a little flustered. "You're Mennonite and I'm Amish," she blurted out.

He chuckled. "I think that's pretty evident, but what's more important than the church we worship in is a commitment to God and to each other. Don't you see—we share the same values,

Leah. I want you to be my wife and the mother of my children."

"Wow." She sank back against the door. "I tell you that this is all too fast—your wanting to date me and your talking about children. You're the one who's not making this easy, Daniel."

"You know I'm right."

"What I know is that, if we did…if we even considered marriage…" *I'd have to give up my church,* she thought, *give up being Amish. I'd have to become Mennonite.* That was the *Plain* way. Usually, a woman joined the man's church, went to live among his people, as her own mother had done. Leah didn't know if she was brave enough…or strong enough to consider such a thing.

"Do you want to walk away without even giving us a chance? What if you live to regret it? What if one day you wish that you could go back and say, 'Yes, Daniel, we should date.'" He paused. "Don't you think this is the best way to know for certain?"

She didn't answer. Was he right? Did she want him to be right? "When God speaks to you, what does He sound like?"

It was dark in the cab of the truck, but she could feel Daniel's intense gaze. "I don't hear Him speak the way I hear you. It's more of a feeling, inside." He touched his chest. "And after

I follow that path, it feels good. It happened when I decided to go to the Univerity of Ohio, instead of the college my parents wanted me to attend. And it happened when I gave up the computer science major to study nursing."

"But if computer science wasn't right for you, then how can you say that God directed you to make the decision to go to that college? God couldn't tell us to do something wrong."

"The college was the right place for me. I just needed some time to figure out what I was supposed to be doing there. Maybe I needed to see more of the world, to try something that didn't fit so I would eventually find my true calling and serve where I was needed most." He turned his face away. "Does that sound too pompous, Leah? Am I too full of myself?"

It sounds like the most honest thing anyone has ever said to me, she thought. "*No.* I'm honored that you'd share it with me."

"So you admit that I'm not completely crazy?" He looked back at her. "So will you go out with me?"

"I said I'd think about it." She shivered, but she wasn't cold. Suddenly, it was hard to breathe. "I don't think I'm ready to take that step yet."

"So, there's no sense in my inviting you to help out at the school bazaar in Felton on Saturday? Since I'm not gainfully employed at the moment,

Uncle Allan is working double-time finding volunteer jobs for me." He hesitated. "Caroline and Leslie won't be there. It would be just you and me and half the congregation of Oak Forest Mennonite Church."

"You want me to go with you Saturday and work at the bazaar?"

"Not as colorful as a Moroccan *souk*, but fun, all the same. I was going to ask you, yes. And I do want you to come with me."

"I don't think that selling crafts and jellies in a room full of people qualifies as a date."

"So you'll go?" he pressed.

"Maybe."

"No maybe, Leah. Be bold. Say yes. You're not a wishy-washy woman. It's what I admired about you from the moment I first laid eyes on you."

She hesitated, then spoke quickly before she chickened out. "All right. I'll come—but…"

"But?"

She held up her finger in warning. "It's not a date. I haven't decided about that yet, and I won't let you push me into anything."

He beamed at her. "I'll pick you up at eight Saturday morning. Is that too early?"

"No, but you don't have to come to the house. I'll walk over to the school where Mam teaches,

Seven Poplars. It's closer to your aunt's. We can meet there."

"You're not going to tell your mother that you're going with me?" he asked.

"It's not our way. Not until…unless we were walking out. Until then, what I do and where I go—within reason—is up to me."

"So, we still aren't *dating* per se, but you will go out with me on Saturday?"

She nodded. "To help at the school bazaar."

He laughed. "It's a deal, Leah Yoder." He pulled back onto the road. "Now, we'd better get that popcorn and get back to Aunt Joyce's before we miss half the movie."

Daniel switched on the radio and turned the dial to a contemporary Christian station. "Do you mind?" he asked. "I really like this song."

"No, it's nice," she said. She wasn't familiar with the singer, but the words were those of a popular hymn and they filled her heart with joy. It was all she could do to keep from tapping her foot to the music.

Among her people, no instrument was allowed except a harmonica, but Leah secretly loved to hear guitar and organ music. She liked the rhythm of some of the country music that Miriam enjoyed, and she appreciated the wholesome songs, but too often the lyrics told stories of drinking or violence or cheating husbands. This music made her feel good inside.

Leah sneaked a peek at Daniel. He was singing along and smiling. The music made him feel good, too.

Daniel glanced at her and caught her looking at him. "I think you're special," he said.

She looked away, feeling bold and shy at the same time. "You too."

Leah arrived at the schoolhouse early Saturday morning, scared, excited, and anxious, all at the same time. All week, she kept replaying in her mind the conversation she and Daniel had had in the cab of his truck on the way to buy popcorn. She kept thinking of how much she loved being with him in the warm darkness, listening to the sweet notes and enthusiastic voices of the artists on the radio...wondering how praising the Lord and giving thanks in a modern tune could possibly be wrong.

Today, she hadn't brought Susanna, and she hadn't asked Mam's permission to go with Daniel. She hadn't even said where she was going, only that she might not be home in time for supper and not to worry.

Rebecca had thrown her a suspicious look, but if Mam had been curious, she hadn't asked. She'd merely slipped her $10 and advised her to wear her bonnet over her *kapp*, because it looked like rain.

Tomorrow was church Sunday, and it would be held at Aunt Martha's home. Mam and her sisters were all preparing food to share at the communal meal after services. Since no cooking could be done on a church Sunday, sandwiches, salads, meat dishes and desserts all had to be made today. Even Johanna would be joining them to help, and Miriam, Ruth and Rebecca would go over to Aunt Martha's to help wash windows and do a final cleaning after the young men moved all the furniture out of the downstairs and brought in the church benches.

Leah had seen Johanna again on Thursday, and she felt a lot better about her sister's situation. Wilmer's sister had been afraid to travel alone with a driver, so Wilmer had gone out to escort her back to Delaware, leaving Johanna and the children at home. Leah had spent Thursday night and most of Friday at her house, and had been relieved to find that Johanna seemed much more like her old self.

"I'm sure that things will be better for us," her sister had said. "With God's help, Wilmer will get better."

"I hope so," Leah had answered. She loved Johanna and the children fiercely, and she wanted things to turn out right for her marriage and her family, but she still wasn't ready to trust Wilmer. He'd promised to change before and had always slipped back to his old, sullen ways.

Without Johanna's husband watching them, Johanna's house had seemed as warm as ever. It was a simple home, but Johanna's quilts and spotless housekeeping made the old house, with its leaky roof and splintered wood floors, seem larger and more welcoming. Her sister was a hard worker, and her curtains were always bleached white and her floors scrubbed and waxed. Leah knew that Johanna struggled to pay her bills and put away a small savings for doctor bills and the occasional medicine the children needed, but she never complained. Strong and vibrant— those were Leah's most powerful memories of her eldest sister, and she had been that way on this visit.

Leah had almost told Johanna about what Daniel had said to her, about thinking she was *the one* and wanting to date her. If any one of her sisters would understand her attraction to Daniel, she thought it might be Johanna. But, in the end, she'd kept her secret. What need was there to discuss Daniel with Johanna if they were simply friends? There would be plenty of time later, if anything came of the relationship.

A truck horn honked and a smiling Daniel pulled into the schoolyard. He jumped out of the cab and came around to open the door for her, looking handsome in a green button-up shirt and brown corduroy trousers. He certainly wouldn't have passed for Amish, but Leah approved. He looked exactly like Daniel, which was right for him…right for the Mennonite boy who had her keeping secrets from her sisters and lying awake at night wondering *what if.*

Chapter Twelve

Leah had been afraid that riding with Daniel to the school bazaar would be awkward and that there might be uncomfortable silences between them. She wasn't a person who needed constant chatter, but this was all so new between her and Daniel. She didn't know if he would feel as though they had to maintain a conversation.

But Leah had always believed that there were other ways to communicate, besides verbally. And sometimes, just being with a person you cared about was what mattered. Some of the best times she had had with her sisters or mother were when they worked side by side in the house or garden or rode in the buggy with only the squeak of the wheels and the clip-clop of the horse's hooves to keep them company. There was a warm satisfaction that came from being so at ease with someone that you could simply enjoy being together without feeling compelled to speak. And to her surprise and delight, sitting beside Daniel as the truck rolled down the country roads was like that.

The day, with all its possibilities, stretched out before her like a table of fresh-baked pies. She was excited at the prospect of meeting new people, of seeing and hearing new things...of doing something different than she'd ever done before. Volunteering for workdays, school auctions, picnics and helping at frolics was familiar. She had taken part in those since she was a small child. But those experiences had always been for another Amish person or family, for someone who shared her faith.

At the food bank and then, later, when they'd packed the boxes for the children's home, she'd felt, somehow, as if this was doing something more. The members of her church were her family. It was natural and right to help your family, but it thrilled her to think that something she could do, in some small way, would help strangers. It made her feel as though she was part of a much bigger family. And with that excitement came shivers of apprehension. What if this was the temptation that the world offered to lure young people away from God's path?

"I'd feel better if I'd picked you up at your house," Daniel said, breaking through her reverie. "It almost seems dishonest, this way…as if we were ashamed of being together, sneaking around."

She smiled at him and shook her head. Daniel was such a good man to worry about her so. "No. It's an Amish thing." She chuckled. "Young people are allowed some freedom. Parents look the other way and pretend not to see what's right in front of them. It isn't really deception because if they told everything, and waited for their parents' permission, how do they learn to make the right choices?"

His green eyes narrowed as he tried to follow her reasoning. "So your mother knows where you are?"

"No, but it's all right with her that she doesn't know."

He exhaled slowly. "I'm still confused, but if you say so, I'll believe you. I'm new to this."

"Driving girls to school bazaars?" she teased. She sat up tall on the seat and looked around. It was a beautiful day, sunny and warm, and she was certain she was going to have fun. "It's new for me, too, being driven in a pickup by a Mennonite boy…alone."

She'd ridden in motor vehicles, of course. She didn't live in an egg basket under a porch. Many times, it was safer and more convenient for Old Order Amish to travel by van. She'd visited relatives in Pennsylvania with her mother since she was eight, and she'd made several trips back and forth to *Grossmama*'s home in Ohio with a hired driver.

"It's nice, though, riding with you," he murmured quietly.

She smiled at him as a small tremor of excitement slid down the nape of her neck. She liked Daniel Brown, and the longer she knew him, the more she liked him. He was such a good man… such a gentle man. For her, he was trouble, and if she had the sense God gave a goose, she would ask him to stop the truck. She'd get out and walk home to her sisters and mother. Spending just one more hour with Daniel was a threat to everything she knew and believed and expected out of life. Instead, she smiled again, settled back against the cushioned seat and asked, "Did you drive cars in Marrakesh?"

He laughed. "Hardly. There don't seem to be many rules of the road in Morocco. I drove in Barcelona, but not in Marrakesh."

Leah looked out at the fields and farmland on either side of the blacktop and tried to imagine the foreign land of Morocco. "What were the people like?"

"Most are warm and friendly," Daniel replied. "Really good people. With an interesting culture. I loved the food there, especially the yogurt and the olives. And the flat bread. There's one called *khobz bishemar* that has onions and chili peppers in it. It's wonderful."

"My mother makes the best bread and biscuits," Leah said, "but I've never tasted any bread with peppers in it." She wondered what Susanna would say if Mam sprinkled her baking powder biscuits with black pepper or chili powder.

She could just picture Susanna wrinkling up her nose and making a face. She wouldn't complain. She'd just slip the food under the table to Jeremiah. Irwin's little terrier was like Irwin. He would eat anything and everything. Neither one ever got fat, and it was a family joke that if you cooked half a cow, Irwin could eat most of it by himself and Jeremiah would finish the rest.

"You'd love the bread. I promise," Daniel went on with enthusiasm. "My mother learned to make it, and we used to have it every Sunday with roasted chicken and vegetables. I can't make the bread, but I make a mean bread pudding with dates and raisins."

"You cook?" She glanced at him in surprise. Mam had always joked that Dat couldn't boil water, and that he'd starve to death without his mother, sisters or wife to cook for him. She didn't know any Amish men who had much skill in the kitchen. Anna said Samuel's children told her that their father always burned the oatmeal and they didn't know it wasn't supposed to be black and crunchy.

"Just eggs and French toast mostly, and sweet muffins and pudding. Stuff I like. Not pie, though. I love pie, especially raisin pie, but I can't make a pie crust fit to eat."

"Pie crust is hard," she agreed. "Anna and Mam make the best. Aunt Jezzy makes hers with a little vinegar, and that's good. Mine are okay." She smiled up at him. "Not bad, but nothing like Anna's."

"Would you make me a raisin pie, if I asked nicely?"

"I might."

On the right side of the road, two boys ran across an open meadow, followed by two puppies. To her left, an English farmer was plowing with a large green tractor. Seagulls swooped down to snatch up bugs and earthworms, and Leah could smell the rich, freshly turned earth. She thought it must be the sweetest scent on earth.

High overhead, she saw a plane headed toward Dover Air Force Base, and she wondered where on earth the people inside had traveled from. Lots of planes passed over her family farm, but most were so high that you never heard a sound. "I know you must have flown in a plane across the Atlantic Ocean to come home from Spain,"

Leah said. "I've always wondered what it would be like, up in the clouds with the birds."

"A little scary if you hit a rough patch, but most of the time, it's good. It's a long trip from Europe—seven hours, give or take, and sometimes longer, once you are waiting to land. When I came back this time, I flew into Cincinnati. That's not a bad airport."

"I can't imagine all the places you've been, all the things you've seen," she said. "Our life in Seven Poplars…it must seem very small to you."

"No." He shook his head. "Not at all. I think… I think that it must be wonderful to feel that God has directed you to live at a slower pace. Money or education can't buy the peace and sense of purpose I see among your people. It must be very satisfying and…" He seemed to search for the right words. "Full of grace."

"But not right for you."

He was quiet for a second, as if he was seriously considering her words. She liked that about Daniel.

"No. I'm not a farmer. I don't feel this pull of the land that I see in others."

"But you find that sense of grace in what you do? In doing God's work in the missions?"

"I try," he admitted. Then he smiled. "Yes, I do. I don't know what tomorrow or the next day will bring, but I believe that if I listen, I'll hear what's right for me. I'll try to do it." He shrugged. "It's all we can do, isn't it? Follow our hearts and try to do our best?"

"Yes," she said. "Try to do our best every day." *And maybe,* she thought, *it was all right to not know what tomorrow would bring...as long as you kept listening for His voice in your heart.*

By ten o'clock, the room that served as both cafeteria and gym to the school was overflowing with students, volunteers and customers. Daniel and Leah had been assigned to the refreshment stand and kitchen, and Leah quickly became the short-order cook when Daniel's methods resulted in a lot of high flames and smoke. Still, they worked well together and quickly figured out a system to serve up hot dogs, hamburgers, scrapple sandwiches, Dutch fried bread, cheesy fries and lemonade without getting in each other's way.

Tables offering used books, toys and baby clothes lined the walls. There were baked goods, plants and crafts for sale as well as a display of local honey and beeswax candles. Jams and jellies vied for space amid jars of homemade spaghetti sauce and a table of birdhouses and feeders. Despite the chaos, the atmosphere in the spacious room was light and airy, with everyone clearly having a good time. Laughing children darted from table to table, and slipped quietly in and out of the adjacent room where a group of high school girls were showing cartoons depicting Bible stories.

Outside, on the playground, there were games, pony rides and a petting zoo. Leah had seen the animals amid the preparations when she and Daniel had arrived. At that point, she wished that she'd brought Susanna with her. Her little sister would have loved it. Susanna had a special fascination with chicks, ducks and other farm animals and the fair atmosphere would have delighted her. But today, selfishly, Leah hadn't wanted to bring her sister. She'd wanted to spend the day with Daniel. She promised herself that she'd do something special with Susanna next week to make it up to her, but today was hers alone.

Later, when the lunchtime rush had passed, two of the teachers took Daniel and her places and Leah went to help sell fresh herbs while Daniel taught a class in CPR. The potted mint and basil and chives went quickly, and soon Leah was down to several flats of cilantro and a planter of rosemary and oregano. Then Daniel's uncle bought those for his wife, and Leah was left to sweep the empty area. Someone had questions about making a quilt, and she was soon involved in a lively discussion with two young, married Mennonite women, one with a small baby. Leah ended up rocking the baby to sleep while one of the teachers showed the mother a new stitch. By the time Daniel came to fetch her, Leah felt that she had made three new friends.

"I was wondering," Daniel said as they walked back to the truck together. "Would you like to go to the beach with me?"

"To the beach?" The bright sunshine had given way to clouds, and soon it would be getting dark. The breeze from the east was cool, and the warmth of the spring day had fled.

"The boardwalk, actually. In Rehoboth. Not that much will be open, but I love the ocean. We could just walk and look at the water and maybe find a place to get a slice of pizza. If you like pizza, that is?"

She laughed. "I love the ocean, and I love pizza. I keep telling Mam we should buy one of those pizza stones. Rebecca and I buy pizza for lunch whenever we go to Spence's and we make our own at home. I'd like to go with you, Daniel…very much, but…"

"But?"

"Remember, this isn't a date—not a real one."

"Well, it could just be two friends looking at the ocean and sharing pizza," he teased.

"Exactly."

And that's what they did. The wind off the water was cool, so Daniel found a jacket of his behind the seat and he lent it to her to throw over her shoulders. They bought a pepperoni pizza with black olives and extra cheese, which Leah insisted on chipping in for, and an extra-large cup of root beer. They found a bench on the boardwalk, and sat and talked until the sun went down, without ever running out of things to say.

They talked about everything, about Ohio and Daniel's cousins and the fun Leah had had at the State Fair with them last summer, about Spanish food, and the best vegetables to put on pizza and how Noah had managed to stow enough grain and hay on the ark to feed all the animals during the Great Flood. Daniel told her about his family and how his father had taught him to juggle rubber balls when he was eight, and Leah told him about sometimes fasting with her family on Thanksgiving Day.

And, finally, when it was growing really dark, neither could put off that it was time to head back to Kent County and home before Leah's mother began to worry about her. "When can I see you again?" Daniel asked as they walked back to where his truck was parked. "Tomorrow?"

"Not tomorrow. Tomorrow is church at Aunt Martha and Uncle Reuben's."

"Maybe I could come," he suggested.

She shook her head. "Amish only. Singing and

prayers and preaching. Five or six hours, maybe more, but definitely no outsiders."

"Is that what I am? An outsider?" He walked beside her, tall and slim and just a little awkward in the fading light. "Because I don't want to be. Not with you."

Not sure what to say, she went on about church. "It's not bad, even though it sounds like a tedious day." She thought for a moment. "It's wonderful, actually. I love church, even when Uncle Reuben forgets pieces of his sermon and hunts for his notes. The singing is like nothing else—we sing in old German. It makes me feel so…so much a part of something special. I love to look around the house and see my friends and neighbors and relatives, babies sleeping, little children playing with their rag dolls, everyone together, wrapped in God's loving arms." She sighed. "It makes me feel so safe."

"I understand exactly what you mean. That's how I feel whenever my family gets together, after Bible School or a holiday dinner." He paused and then said softly. "I miss them, Mom and Dad, and my brothers and sisters. Growing up in another country, I think you get really close to your family. Most of them are up in Canada now. I hope I'll get to see them before I go to my next assignment."

"You couldn't have gone there with them?"

"I suppose I could have, if I'd asked. But they didn't need a nurse, and there are other places where the people have no available medical care. It only seems fair that I go where I can do the most good."

She nodded. She didn't want to think about him going away and never seeing him again, but she'd known all along that Daniel was only here for a short time. There was no way they could continue their friendship after he left Delaware, not really. "And after the worship service, we have a communal meal," she continued. "The host is supposed to feed everyone, but most families bring food to share."

"It sounds like a good time," he agreed.

"It is. I always feel so clean afterwards, as though I left all my troubles on the floor by my bench."

"I'm sorry I can't come, then," he said.

"Me, too."

"You would be welcome at a Mennonite church service."

She nodded, actually saddened by the idea that she couldn't invite him to church. "It just isn't our way, Daniel. We are a people apart."

"I wish you weren't," he said. "Or I wish there were some way we could bring both our faiths together, so that everyone would understand how much alike we really are."

"There *is* something you would be welcome at," she said. "On Wednesday evening, the Gleaners are going to repair a chicken house and fence in the poultry yard for a family. Anyone can go. Rebecca and Miriam and Susanna and I are going to whitewash the chicken house and help with refreshments. Samuel's going to lend his team, and Charley's going to drive us in a straw wagon. If you'd like to come, we can always use an extra pair of hands."

"A hay ride and a chicken fence." Daniel laughed. "Sounds like fun."

"Then it's settled." They were walking on the sidewalk now, almost to the truck. "Mam is hosting the Gleaners for a haystack supper at five. Come and eat with us. There will be so many people here, no one will notice one extra Mennonite missionary."

"I've never eaten a haystack before, but you can count on me to try anything."

She laughed. "You'll like it, I promise. It has onions, but no chilies, and definitely no figs."

"And I suppose this isn't a date you're inviting me on, even though it is a hayride?"

"*Ne,* Daniel," she teased. "Not a date, and not even a hayride. Straw is a lot less prickly when it gets down the back of your neck."

He opened his arms wide. "In that case, how can I refuse?"

Chapter Thirteen

Leah shivered with anticipation as she saw Daniel turn his truck into the school driveway and get out. The swings, where she usually waited for him, were half-hidden by the trees and the corner of the schoolhouse. She could see him, but he couldn't see her, and it gave her a secret thrill to watch him walk toward her through the tall grass.

It was mid-May, and the Seven Poplars Amish School had closed for the summer. In the past few weeks, since the children no longer came every day, the weeds had begun to take over the playground and creep up the side of the neat white building. She'd have to remember to mention to Mam that the grass needed cutting, if she could think of some way to bring it up without admitting that she'd been meeting Daniel here. The school had a three-rail fence around it. Maybe Irwin could lead one or two of the heifers over so that they could crop the grass.

"Leah?" Daniel called. "Are you here?"

"I'm here, Daniel," she answered. Just saying his name made her happy. Daniel made her happy. Despite the unsuitability of their friendship, she didn't want to think about not seeing him…about what it had been like before she'd known Daniel. She didn't want to think about him going away.

Leah smiled and waved. She was seated on one of the swings, and now she gave herself a small push with her feet. She wanted to leap off the swing and run into his arms. She wanted to hug him tightly, but, of course, she wouldn't. As long as they weren't doing anything to be ashamed of, as long as her behavior was properly *Plain*, she didn't have to feel guilty for seeing him secretly. Did she?

Daniel stopped directly in front of her. "We need to talk," he said.

She looked up at him and her stomach clenched. Something was wrong. Gooseflesh rose on the back of her neck. "What is it?" she asked.

He reached out and caught hold of the ropes. The swing stopped and she half rose and then sat down hard on the seat. The schoolyard was suddenly still. In the distance, she could hear peepers and the cooing of a mourning dove. It was a sad sound, and she felt a sudden wash of apprehension. Was this the moment when everything changed between them? Moisture clouded her vision.

"What's wrong?"

"It's been a couple of weeks. It's time to have this out, Leah," he said. Daniel's tone was firm. "We've been avoiding it too long."

She blinked away the tears. *No,* she thought. *I don't want to lose him.*

His voice grew husky. "We can't keep doing this, Leah," he said, taking the swing next to her. "You know we can't. It's not honest."

She twisted so that she could look into his eyes. "What's not honest? Us seeing each other? Being friends?"

"We're more than friends. We both know that." He took a deep breath. "I need to talk to your mother, to tell her that we're serious. It's time, Leah."

He was right. She knew he was right, but she still wasn't ready. She gripped the ropes harder. The swing wasn't moving, but she felt as if the ground was far away and she might fall off, and keep on falling. "I never meant to be dishonest," she said. The tight prickling sensation behind her eyes grew stronger and she was afraid that she was going to burst into tears and shame herself.

For the past few weeks, they'd been seeing each other several times a week. She'd kept up the pretense, insisting that they weren't dating, and maybe they hadn't been, at first. But they were now. By Amish standards, Mennonite standards and probably even English standards. And she couldn't bear for it to end.

"Say it," he said quietly. "We're dating."

She took a breath, but she didn't have enough air. She felt dizzy. The ground was still so far beneath her feet, and the warm May twilight was taking on a damp chill fast.

"You have to admit it, Leah. To me and to yourself."

She nodded. "Yes," she agreed. "We're dating."

"All right." Some of the lines smoothed around his eyes and he gave her the hint of a smile. "So, if we're dating...if we're *walking out together*, then it's time we told someone. I want to make my intentions clear to your mother and to my aunt and uncle."

She nibbled at her bottom lip.

"You know I'm right," he said.

"It's not easy...what you're asking me to do," she murmured.

"But we can't go on like this." He reached across the distance between them and took her hand in his. "I've tried to reason this out. I've tried to be logical, but all I can think of is how much I care about you and how inappropriate this is."

"Because of who I am?" she asked. "Because we…we come from different faiths?"

"Because we're not being honest with our families." He paused and went on, his words tumbling over one another in his haste. "I've prayed over it, Leah. I'm certain that God wants us to be together, that He wants us to marry. But we have to do this right. We can't hurt the people who love us most just because we're a little scared."

"You want to tell everyone how you feel about me, but you haven't asked me how I feel about you," she said. "You have to ask me."

"Okay. I'm asking you."

She shook her head. "That's the problem, Daniel. I'm not sure of how I feel."

"But you care for me?"

"Of course, I do. You know I do. But…" *Why was she such a coward?*

He nodded. "If you're still unsure, I can understand that. It's all happened so fast. But…I have to know…is there a possibility? Do you think I'm a man you *could* love? A man who could make you happy?"

"I think so," she said softly.

"Do you?" He squeezed her hand. "I'm certain of how I feel. I love you and I want you to be my wife."

"I've prayed, too," she answered, holding onto his hand with all her might. "But God's not answering me. I can't hear Him. It can't be just you who's sure. It has to be me, too. I have to be certain this is right…right for both of us."

Daniel nodded. "I agree. Pushing you into something you don't want is the last thing I'd ever do. But you must have some idea of how you feel…inside."

"I do," she said. "I think I'm in love with you, but…"

"But?"

She smiled at him through her tears. "It's hard, because I've never been in love before. It's hard to know if it's real or just…wishing."

"Do you trust me, Leah?"

She nodded. "Yes." Of that, she was certain. She trusted Daniel Brown with all her heart, utterly…completely.

"Does being with me make you feel happy or unhappy?"

"Happy. But for us to…to marry, it would mean…"

He stood and gathered her in his arms. She leaned against him, soaking up his strength and warmth. *This is right,* she thought. *This must be love I feel.* And just being near him gave her the courage to say what had to be said.

"If we were to marry, one of us would have to change our faith," she said.

"I'd become Amish for you," Daniel said. "I would if I could. If I were free, I'd give up nursing and learn to plow fields and grow wheat, if that would make you happy. But I'm not free, Leah. I've already given my promise."

"To whom?" she asked.

"To God. I know it sounds...sounds prideful, that God spoke to me. But I believe He has. I believe that God's called me to serve Him. I can't refuse Him. Can you understand that? As much as I love you, I can't turn my back on the promise I made to God."

"Of course, you can't," she said. "I wouldn't want you to. But that's why I have to be absolutely certain. If I marry you, I'll be like Ruth, in the Bible. I'll go with you, wherever you go, and I'll worship as you worship. Your people will be my people, and my children raised in your church. If I say *yes*, Daniel, it will be with a fully willing heart, not halfway."

He stepped back and raised her chin so that he could stare into her eyes. "You are the most wonderful woman in the whole world," he whispered, "the only woman I'd ever ask to be my wife. And no matter what your answer is, I'll love you for the rest of my life, and only you."

And as he said those words, Leah felt a loosening in her chest and a sudden rush of joy. There was no voice in her head, no jolt of electricity, just a sense of release and warm happiness that made her certain. "Yes," she said. "You're right, Daniel. It's time my mother knew of our decision. Only…only, I need to speak to her first. I've been acting like a child. I haven't been fair to her, and I'm going to tell Mam."

"Tell her what?" he urged.

She smiled at him with all her heart. "Tell her that a very good young man has done me the honor of asking me to be his wife."

A wide, silly grin split his face. "Get in the truck, Leah. We're going right now to find her."

"Oh, no," she said, suddenly giggly with relief. "Not tonight. Tomorrow. I have to have time to break this to her gently. Otherwise, she might take your head off with her wooden spoon."

"She can't hit me," he protested, still grinning. "You're peace-loving people."

"Mam may be peace-loving," Leah said, "but when it comes to protecting her family, she can be pretty scary."

Leah slipped into the kitchen just as the rest of the family was sitting down to supper. Aunt Jezzy looked up and smiled. "Here's our girl, Hannah," she said.

Susanna waved. "*Grossmama* isn't here to-night," she said. "Samuel came to get her."

Rebecca carried a pitcher of iced tea to the table as Leah washed her hands, dried them on a towel and slid into her place at the table. Irwin caught her attention and rolled his eyes. Leah ignored him and addressed her mother. "The ham smells delicious, Mam."

"Anna sent cinnamon buns with Samuel when he came for *Grossmama*," Susanna said. "And strawberry pie."

Leah remembered that her grandmother was spending the night at Anna's tonight. They were in the process of moving *Grossmama*'s belongings to Anna and Samuel's, and Anna had felt that it might make it easier for *Grossmama* if they made the change gradually. They'd been inviting her to supper several times a week, and having the senior bus drop her off there on the days she went to the center.

Irwin cleared his throat, and Leah looked around, realizing that everyone had bowed their heads in preparation for silent grace. Speaking to Mam about Daniel would have to wait. As much as she might want to get it over with, Leah knew that mealtime was family time, and not the place to announce that she wanted to turn Mennonite, marry Daniel Brown and go off to be a missionary.

Leah had no doubt that her mother loved her, and that she'd support her decision in the end, but it was all the fussing in between that had her worried. And just thinking about the explosion to come made her sister Anna's feather-light cinnamon rolls go down like lead.

Supper was usually earlier, but tonight Mam had outdone herself and they were eating late. There was fresh asparagus, coleslaw, turnips whipped with potatoes, cold fried chicken, chow-chow, pickled beets, deviled eggs, and steamed cabbage with caraway seeds to go with the smoked ham. Irwin ate enough for two grown men, but Leah could only swallow a few bites.

What would she do if her mother refused to speak to Daniel or if she cried? Mam never cried, at least almost never, but when she did, it was a disaster. Even her mother's temper was better than tears. And it would be worse if she called in Ruth and Miriam to back her up. How could Leah possibly explain her decision to all of them at once? And she could expect no help from Rebecca. Leah wished she'd asked Daniel to give her a week, rather than a day, to explain things to her mother.

Without *Grossmama* at the supper table, Aunt Jezebel was jovial and bursting with stories about Dat's childhood. She was in the middle of a particularly funny one involving a visiting bishop and Dat's pet billy goat when Jeremiah flew out from under the table and began to bark furiously.

"I think someone's here," Mam said.

"I'll see who it is," Leah offered, going to the screen door.

"Mam!"

The voice was Johanna's, and as Leah rushed out onto the porch, she could see at once that her sister had been crying. "Johanna, what's wrong?"

Johanna stood there, shaking from head to foot and clutching little Jonah by the hand. Jonah was white-faced and looked scared to death. He was bareheaded, his red hair sweaty and sticking out in tufts, his bare feet dusty.

"Wilmer," Johanna said, on the verge of breaking down. She shook her head. "I've never seen him this bad."

Their mother swung the kitchen door wide. "Come in, child," she said, gathering Jonah up in her arms. "Susanna, take this tired little boy. Wash him up and give him some strawberry pie."

Jonah began to sob and reach out to Johanna, but Mam cradled him against her breast. "Shhh, shhh, it's all right. Go with Aunt Susanna like a big boy. Your mam's right here."

"Where's Katy?" Leah demanded. Johanna didn't stir out of her house without the baby... without either of her two children. "Is she—"

Johanna threw a meaningful glance at her

small son, and Leah nodded. "Susanna," she said with false cheerfulness. "See if you can find out who's under that dirty face."

"It's Jonah," Susanna said.

Mam smiled at her and passed the boy into her arms. Murmuring to him, Susanna carried him out of the kitchen. "Irwin," Mam said sternly. "Best you go out to the barn and check on that milk cow. I think her calf may be coming before morning."

"It's too early for that calf," Irwin said, clearly bewildered by whatever was going on. "It won't be for another two weeks or so."

"You heard Hannah," Aunt Jezzy said. "Best you go and keep an eye on her."

"But my supper…"

"Take your pie and milk with you," Mam said. "You and Jeremiah stay with the cow until I send someone for you."

As soon as Irwin was out of the house, Leah drew Johanna to a chair and the rest of them gathered around her. Anger flared in Leah's chest as she saw the puffy eye and the bruises on her sister's arms, injuries that had obviously been made by a man's hard hands.

"Now, tell us what's happened," she urged her sister.

"Wilmer got mad. It was over nothing, but he got madder and madder. Jonah started crying, and Wilmer…" A single tear rolled down Johanna's sweat-streaked cheek. "He…he grabbed me and shook me. Then he picked up Jonah and threw him at me. He told us to get out." She choked back a sob. "He wouldn't let me take Katy. He said Katy was his and I couldn't have her!" Another tear rolled down her cheek.

Without a word, Aunt Jezebel brought ice wrapped in a washcloth and pressed it against Johanna's black eye.

"What about Wilmer's sister?" Mam asked. "How could she stand by while this happened? Wasn't she there?"

Johanna nodded. "She's there. She has Katy. I think she was scared too. He doesn't usually get like that around his own people. I didn't want to leave Katy, but I was afraid of what he might do. He was so angry…and I didn't do anything. It was about nothing at all…a crack in his coffee cup that's been there for weeks. Jonah had nothing to do with the cup. Wilmer just got so mad, so fast."

Leah put her arm around Johanna's shoulders. "It's him," she said. "Wilmer. Of course it's not Jonah's fault."

"Wilmer wouldn't believe me. He said Jonah broke his mug…that I spoiled him…that he had to spend his life working for a willful brat. He was so angry that it scared me." She looked at their mother with tear-filled eyes. "I want my baby, Mam. I had to get Jonah here, where it's safe, but I'm going back for my Katy."

"Ne." Mam stiffened. "You will stay here with your sisters and Aunt Jezebel. I'm going to fetch Samuel. He'll get the baby. Wilmer might not let you have Katy, but he won't stand against Samuel."

"I'll come with you," Leah offered, trying to hide her own apprehension. "I'll hitch up the buggy." She didn't want to think of small Katy in that house with her angry father. How frightened she must be without Johanna and Jonah. Wilmer's sister was kind enough, but she was a meek and soft-spoken woman, not strong enough to stand up to him when he was in one of his moods.

Mam shook her head. "I'll cut across the field," she said. "It's faster. We can take Samuel's horse and buggy. You stay here with Johanna. Your sister needs you."

"I can't just sit here and wait," Johanna protested. She pushed the washcloth away.

"You can and you will," their mother insisted, "Wilmer is not well. You, of all people, know that. He could be dangerous. We will take no chances with you and your children. Samuel will know how to manage Wilmer."

"Did I do wrong to leave her?" Johanna asked tearfully. "I didn't know what to do, but I thought—"

"You did right," Leah said, trying to remain calm. "Exactly right. We have you and Jonah safe, and now Mam and Samuel will go and get your Katy."

Chapter Fourteen

It was two days before things calmed down enough at home for Leah to approach her mother concerning Daniel. Mam was picking strawberries in the new berry bed at the far corner of the garden. It was a brilliant morning, with a blue, blue sky, sunshine and enough of a breeze to send the blades of the big windmill spinning. As she walked across the lawn toward her mother, Leah could smell the sweet scent of honeysuckle from the hedgerow, where a mockingbird warbled a joyous song.

How can I think of leaving all this behind? she wondered. Would she ever find the peace and happiness she'd known here in this quiet corner of Kent County? Was she making the biggest mistake of her life?

She thought back to her meeting with Daniel at the schoolhouse the morning after Johanna had come home with the black eye and only one of her children. As Mam had assured them, Samuel had taken care of Wilmer, or at least he'd solved the immediate problem of getting little Katy back. According to Mam, Wilmer had been almost ashamed of himself when the two of them had arrived at Johanna's home. Wilmer denied roughly grabbing Johanna, but he'd handed over a sleeping Katy without a fuss.

As Leah explained to Daniel, Samuel had taken Johanna's plight to the bishop and to the church elders, and everyone agreed that she was better off at Mam's until Wilmer could work through his crisis. As much as Daniel wanted to be open about their *walking out together,* he understood that Johanna's troubles were much more pressing. But Leah had promised to talk to her mother as soon as possible, and this morning seemed like the best time.

"Leah! Leah!" Susanna waved to her from the clothesline where she was hanging out towels and children's clothes to dry in the sunshine. "See our scarecrow!" she shouted.

"It's lovely!" Leah called back.

Susanna and Irwin had made a new scarecrow to keep the blackbirds out of the strawberry patch. They'd taken old clothes, good for nothing but scrub cloths, stuffed them with straw, and plopped a ragged bonnet on top. Then

Susanna had added sparkly streamers of aluminum foil and strung can lids to the broomstick that served as arms. It was a good scarecrow, and Leah didn't know who was more pleased, Susanna or Irwin. It was Dat who'd taught his girls how to make scarecrows, and back in Pennsylvania, when he was a boy, Dat had made such funny ones that he'd been able to sell them to the English for their gardens.

Leah reached the edge of the strawberry patch and started picking near the scarecrow, in the next row over from her mother. The berries were fat and ripe, bursting with juice, and it was all Leah could do not to eat more than she put in her split-oak basket. What she had to tell her mother was daunting, and she concentrated on filling her container as she gathered her nerve.

For the past two days, Mam's face had shown the worry she felt over Johanna's disastrous marriage, but this morning, here in the garden with the birds singing and the sun shining, she looked years younger. And thinking of the possibility of her own marriage to Daniel, Leah wondered if Mam would ever take a new husband.

Thinking of her mother marrying someone was a little disturbing. However, it was expected. Few Old Amish widows in their forties remained widows for long, but it would take a lot of getting used to. With her daughters leaving to set up homes of their own, Mam and Susanna would soon need help running the farm. But she had her own way of doing things, and a new husband might bring as many problems as solutions.

Leah retrieved a particularly large cluster of strawberries and tried to think of the best way to approach her mother. Once she'd told Mam, there would be no going back, and maybe that was part of her reluctance. She did love Daniel. She was certain she did, but what she wasn't sure of was her ability to leave home—to leave her family and her entire way of life to go off and be with someone else. The farm, her mother and sisters, even Irwin, would always be a part of her. What kind of a wife and partner would she be for Daniel? Was she doing the right thing for both of them? Doubts haunted the shadowy corners of her mind.

"You have something to say to me, daughter?" Mam asked, startling Leah so badly that she dropped a strawberry and it rolled into the center of the open space between the rows. "You've been following me around all morning with that guilty expression on your face."

"Me?"

"Ya," Mam said. "You, Leah. You may be a woman grown, but in some ways you'll never change. Remember when you poured the big crock of honey in Aunt Martha's church bonnet?"

"I was four and I thought it would make her sweet," Leah protested. So long as she lived, her sisters or Aunt Martha would never let her live it down.

"You may as well come clean. What have you done now?"

Leah glanced away, then back at her mother. "This is more serious than a child's prank, Mam. It's Daniel. Daniel Brown. We're…we're seeing each other."

Mam set down her strawberry basket and straightened her back. "More than that, I'd say. And isn't this a little late to be telling me?"

Leah felt the sting of her mother's disapproval in her gaze. "You knew?"

"I knew. It isn't like you, Leah, to sneak around. But a Mennonite boy? Have you thought what this would mean? Not just for you, but for our whole family? How your sisters will feel if anything comes of it?"

Leah looked at the ground, suddenly ashamed. "I didn't mean to hurt you," she said. "I just didn't know that I'd feel this way about Daniel."

"Is it serious? Has he asked to court you?"

Leah nodded. "He has…and I've said I would…let him, I mean."

Her mother closed her eyes for a second and hugged herself, rubbing her arms with her fingertips. "I always wondered what I'd say if one of my girls came to me and said that," she said. "I wondered, but I never had the answer. I still don't."

Leah raised her chin and looked her mother eye to eye. They were the same height. "I think I love him, Mam."

"Love of a man is one thing, daughter. Living a lifetime with him is another. Daniel Brown is Mennonite. I know you've considered what that would mean."

"A hundred times. Every waking minute."

"And you think you could give up your faith for him?"

"Why shouldn't she follow her heart, Mam?" Johanna walked from the grape arbor toward them. She didn't seem shocked; her sister must have been standing only a few yards away, listening to their conversation.

"This is between Leah and me," Mam chided. "You shouldn't interfere."

"Why not? She's my sister, isn't she? I owe her the wisdom of my experience, too." Johanna turned to look into Leah's face. "Do what's right for you. If you don't, you may live to regret it."

"Johanna," Mam said. "Don't—"

"Don't what?" Johanna cried emotionally. "Don't say what we all know is the truth?"

"You're upset," Mam soothed. "Things are bad now between you and your husband, but—"

"I was a fool," Johanna said. "I turned down the man I loved over a foolish misunderstanding. And now, I'll never be happy again." She took hold of Leah's arm, tears filling her eyes. "Don't make the same mistake. Daniel's a good man. So what if he's a Mennonite? Don't they worship the same God? If you love him, marry him, Leah. Because the one thing you don't want is to be tied into a marriage with the wrong man."

Mam fussed, but in the end, she softened enough to invite Daniel to dinner that night. The meal was awkward, with long periods of silence and black looks from Rebecca and Ruth, but as the days passed, the family seemed to tolerate having Daniel among them. Leah continued to attend church with Mam and her sisters on alternate Sundays, but she also began to take part in Mennonite worship services, such as a weekly Bible school for adults. Daniel's aunt and uncle were polite, if not enthusiastic, about the two of them keeping company.

"It will take time for them to accept us," Daniel said soothingly. "All of them."

Leah had her doubts. Her grandmother and Aunt Martha took no pains to hide their disapproval of the match, and Bishop Atlee became a regular visitor to the Yoder farm. Through it all, she and Daniel continued to volunteer for the food bank and to help with Amish work frolics, but generally, the Amish community—other than Leah's immediate family and Samuel—ignored Daniel.

It wasn't easy to be at odds with people she'd known and loved all her life, but the longer she and Daniel knew each other, the more Leah felt that he was right for her. Of her sisters, only Johanna—who remained at Mam's with her children—seemed totally supportive of the romance.

"How long will you have together before you have to make a final decision?" Johanna asked, one afternoon when they were making strawberry jam. Susanna had taken Jonah and Katy outside to play, and Mam and Rebecca had gone next door to Ruth's to help her and Miriam can asparagus.

"There's no way to know," Leah answered. "He expects to get word soon, though, and then he could be sent anywhere. It will probably be back to Spain or maybe even Mexico. Daniel speaks Spanish, and that would make working in a medical clinic easier for him and for his patients."

Johanna used pot holders to transfer the hot jars of jam from the counter to a butcher-block table near the window to cool. So far, they had finished thirty-two pints, and the rows of ball jars shone like jewels in the afternoon sun.

"So, if you do marry him, you'll have to go away for a long time?"

"It could be as long as a year." Leah smiled at her sister. "I can't imagine what it would be like—living in a foreign country and learning to cook and eat the different foods. But wherever we are, there will be a Mennonite community. It may be small, but we'll be able to have our own worship services and celebrate holidays as if we were home."

"So you have decided to marry him?" Johanna arched an auburn brow. "You're certain?"

"Almost. Yes, I think I am." She didn't want to admit to Johanna that she was still hoping to hear God's answer to her prayers loud in her ears. She thought she knew what God's plan was for her—Daniel certainly was sure of it. But, so far, she hadn't received any personal messages. Maybe it was prideful, but she was still waiting and listening. "Almost," she repeated. "I know I love Daniel. It's not Daniel, it's me I still have doubts about."

"You wonder if you have the courage to take a leap of faith," Johanna said, speaking aloud the words Leah had been thinking.

"Yes," she admitted.

"Have you prayed about it? Asked for the Lord's guidance?"

Leah nodded. "But…" She sighed. "I don't think God has heard me."

Johanna wiped her hands on her apron, went to the table, and began to write the date on the labels for the jars of jam. "He always hears us," she said. "Sometimes, I think we don't listen when He speaks to us."

Leah approached the table and leaned on the back of a chair. Her sister's writing was bold and clear as she used the permanent marker to fill in one pretty label after another. Leah and Rebecca had picked out the labels from a catalog, and they showed a basket overflowing with fruit. They made the ordinary canning jars look special and attracted customers at Spence's.

"Why did you speak up to Mam for me?" Leah asked. "When I talked to you before…about Daniel, I thought you were warning me to stay away from him."

Johanna's blue eyes sparkled with moisture. "It was my duty as a big sister and a member of the church. If you had listened to me and decided not to see Daniel again, then your love for him wouldn't have been more than a flirtation. But if you're willing to go against all of us, he must be right for you."

"Is that what I'm doing, Johanna? Going against my family?"

"Ne." Johanna smiled and shook her head.

"Not me, and in the end, not Mam, either. Remember, she was born Mennonite. They must be good people if she was one of them. But I'll expect to get letters from you every week with foreign stamps on them, letters that tell me everything you do and everything wonderful you see."

"Thank you." Leah hugged her. "You don't know how much it means to me—to have you on my side."

"We're all on your side," Johanna said. "It just depends on where you're standing." She rose. "Now, let's get this jam put away and start on the birthday cakes for Aunt Jezzy. I think we'll need four, at least."

Leah nodded. "At least. Daniel and Irwin can eat a whole one between them. What kind are we making?"

"With all these strawberries?" Johanna shrugged. "Strawberry shortcake. What else?" Leah laughed and went to get the big sheet cake pans from the pantry.

The following day, Anna and Samuel, *Grossmama*, and the children, Aunt Martha, Uncle Reuben, and Dorcas, Roman and Fannie and their little ones, as well as Ruth and Miriam, Eli and Charley were all coming to share a birthday supper on the lawn. Samuel had put a pig on to roast over hot coals at six in the morning, and Anna was preparing baked beans and coleslaw. Charley and Eli were in charge of setting up tables and benches outside. Miriam was making a huge fruit salad, and Ruth had promised enough potato salad to feed the whole church.

Leah, Rebecca, Susanna and Johanna would cook the rest of the food this afternoon. Leah couldn't wait to have Daniel enjoy a meal with her extended family. She was even looking forward to his meeting Aunt Martha. She was Aunt Jezebel's niece, and could hardly be left out of the birthday party. Besides, maybe once Aunt Martha got to know him, she wouldn't be so critical of their courting. It wasn't likely, Leah thought, but you never knew. Mam kept saying that under her crusty exterior, Aunt Martha had a good heart. If that was true, her shell must be pretty tough.

As it happened, Aunt Martha didn't come.

"Mam slipped in the wash water and pulled her back," Dorcas explained. "She said to tell your mother and Aunt Jezzy that she's sorry, but she thought it would be best if she just went to bed with a hot water bottle."

"Ya," Uncle Reuben chimed on. "But she said be sure and bring her a plate. You know how she likes roast pork."

"And she wants a big slice of birthday cake,"

Dorcas finished. "Or two if you have extra. Her appetite isn't quite what it used to be and she fancies a little cake now and then."

Leah glanced at Johanna, and her sister rolled her eyes. It was all Leah could do not to giggle. Aunt Martha always said she wasn't hungry, but Mam said Aunt Martha could eat more than Anna and Samuel put together, and she always wanted a plate of leftovers to take home. Not that anyone minded. Mam always had enough food to feed the county, and today was no exception.

Eli put Daniel to work helping with the tables, while Leah and her sisters carried out platters of food. Samuel brought his roast pig in his daughters' pony cart and drove it right around to the grassy backyard. The pork smelled wonderful, almost as good as the bushel of yeast rolls that Fannie had baked that afternoon.

There was a bustle as Mam supervised the food, and Charley and Irwin carried out two armchairs for either end of the tables. One was for *Grossmama*, and the other for Aunt Jezebel. Leah's aunt was as giggly as a girl. She kept saying that she couldn't believe all this fuss was for her or that she was sixty years old today.

"I remember when I was ten," she said excitedly. "My uncle took me fishing to a lake and we went in a boat. I caught the biggest fish and my mother cooked it for my supper."

Eventually, everyone was seated, grace was finished, and the eating, laughing and talking began. Daniel sat directly across from Leah, between Eli and Charley, and it was hard for Leah to take a bite with him watching her. *He fits in,* she thought. *He may be different, but he fits in.* Here, for the first time, she could feel her family and friends slowly lowering the fences.

Halfway through the meal, Rebecca stood up and read a poem she had written about Aunt Jezebel. Aunt Jezzy's face turned beet-red and she covered her face with her hands, but it was easy to see that she was pleased. Leah smiled at Mam, so glad that her mother had thought to honor Dat's aunt's special day. Not everyone understood Aunt Jezebel or knew how deeply she felt things. Some even said she was touched. It was true that she had her odd ways and that she'd never married. But Leah loved her.

"I'm thirsty," *Grossmama* said loudly from the far end of the table. "Is there more lemonade? My glass is empty."

Rebecca leaned close to Leah's ear and whispered. "She probably isn't thirsty. She probably doesn't like all the attention Aunt Jezzy is getting."

"I'll get some more from the house," Johanna offered. She rose and put little Katy into Mam's lap. "I'll just be a minute."

Roman began a story and Samuel had funny comments to make. Soon, everyone was laughing.

"Where's that Johanna with my lemonade?" *Grossmama* demanded.

"I'll go see what's keeping her," Leah offered.

"Probably spilled the whole pitcher," her grandmother grumbled. "Bring me water if there's no more lemonade. Better yet, buttermilk. You must have buttermilk. It's good for my stomach."

Daniel got to his feet. "I'll come with you," he said. "In case you need to carry anything."

"No, stay here and finish your supper," Leah said. If they went off together it would *look* as if they'd planned this—as if it was a scheme to be alone together. As long as Daniel was at the table, even Samuel couldn't think they were doing anything wrong.

Instead of going in through the back, Leah walked around the house. Out front, she saw a buggy standing in the middle of the yard— Wilmer's buggy. The horse was white with sweat, foam bubbled from his nostrils and his head hung down. Worse, the animal's knees were scraped and bloody. Someone had driven him hard, so hard that he'd fallen on the gravel and injured himself.

Fear sent goose bumps rising across the tops

of her arms. She quickened her pace toward the house, and as she neared the porch, she could hear Wilmer's angry voice.

"You didn't invite me!" he shouted. "A family gathering and you forget your husband!" Something heavy crashed to the floor. "You're coming home with me! Where you belong!"

Leah ran up onto the porch and flung open the kitchen door. Wilmer rushed after Johanna, but she ducked around the table. He made a dash to grab her, but Leah seized the nearest object she could find—a broom—and thrust it between Wilmer's ankles. He tripped and fell, giving Johanna and Leah time to run out onto the porch.

Wilmer came after them, roaring like a bull. His face was white, his eyes bulging. Leah caught the stink of alcohol radiating off his dirty clothing. Johanna's husband looked like a tramp. One suspender hung loose, and his shoes were untied. His hands and arms were streaked with mud.

"Go home!" Johanna cried. "You're drunk, and I'm not going anywhere with you."

He dove at her. She leaped off the porch and Leah darted between them. "Leave her alone," she shouted. Wilmer brushed her away with one swing of his arm.

From somewhere, the dogs had come. Jeremiah circled Wilmer, barking furiously, while the Shetland sheepdog crouched, growling. The dogs had never been hostile to Wilmer before. Leah sensed that they knew he wasn't himself.

"Go home!" Johanna repeated. "You're sick. I'm staying here with my children until you get help."

Wilmer raised a meaty fist and advanced on her.

"Run, Johanna!" Leah shouted. She ducked behind Wilmer, grabbed the rope that hung from the big iron bell and rang it as hard as she could.

Wilmer beat Johanna to the gate, and he trapped her in the corner of the picket fence. She hitched up her skirt, put a foot on the cross-rung and attempted to climb over the fence, but he caught her bonnet string and yanked her head back. Her bonnet slipped off, and she dodged around him, running for the open gate. She dashed through just ahead of Wilmer.

Still shouting, he pounded after her, but, suddenly, Daniel appeared. He stepped in front of Wilmer and Johanna's husband stopped short. "Get out of my way!" he threatened. "This is no business of yours, Mennonite!"

"Put your hand down," Daniel said quietly. "This is no way to treat your wife."

Wilmer put it down, all right. He smashed his fist into Daniel's jaw. Daniel fell back onto the ground, but he scrambled up and put himself between a weeping Johanna and Wilmer again. "You don't want to do this," Daniel said, rubbing his chin. "Violence solves nothing. Better to talk this—"

Wilmer swung at him again. Leah screamed, but Daniel weaved out of Wilmer's reach. "You need help," Daniel said calmly. "I'm a nurse. I can help you get the medical attention you need."

Behind Leah, people were gathering: Mam, Roman, her sisters and their husbands. Eli and Charley rushed forward and seized Wilmer. He cursed in German and tried to shake them off, but they were too strong for him. After a minute or two, Wilmer sagged to his knees, weeping. "She's my wife," he wailed. "It's her duty. She has to come home. Tell her, Samuel. Tell Johanna she has to come home."

Samuel strode forward and knelt in the dirt in front of Wilmer. He put his broad hands on Wilmer's shoulders. "Shh, shh, brother," he said, before glancing at Roman. "Bring your buggy. Not his buggy, yours. His horse is in no shape to be driven. We'll take him to Bishop Atlee."

Johanna threw herself into Mam's arms. Her shoulders were shaking, but she wasn't crying.

"It's all right," Mam said. "You're safe. The children are safe."

Everyone stared in silence as Eli and Charley and Samuel ushered a blubbering Wilmer into Roman's buggy. "Did you see his horse?" Miriam said. "It's a disgrace. He must have tried to run him on the blacktop." She and Rebecca were already unhitching the trembling animal from its traces.

"Poor Boomer," Johanna crooned. "I need to—"

"Go with Mam," Ruth said. "Miriam and Susanna will look after the horse."

Leah moved away from her family to where Daniel stood, still rubbing his jaw. "You were wonderful," she said. "If you hadn't come, I don't know what would have happened."

"I wouldn't have hit him," Daniel said. "I don't believe in physical violence, but he wouldn't have hurt you or your sister again. I promise you that."

She looked up into his determined green eyes and felt a surge of what could only be admiration. "But you got hurt," she said. "Your poor jaw."

He shrugged. "Nothing serious. I've gotten lots worse playing soccer."

Chapter Fifteen

"Wilmer's problems are too serious for your church elders to deal with," Daniel said, later that evening, as he prepared to leave the Yoder farm. Leah had walked to the pickup with him, and they were standing close in the twilight. "He needs professional help. He's suffering from depression; from what you've said, it sounds like he's been suffering from it for some time. And your sister should file charges against him. I don't understand why Samuel advises against it."

"He's her husband, and he didn't hit her. Not this time," Leah answered. "You prevented that from happening. The bishop won't allow it to happen again. And Johanna and the children are staying here with Mam indefinitely, so Wilmer won't have another opportunity to hurt her."

Daniel gritted his teeth, trying not to allow his impatience to show. How could he make Leah understand how grave the situation was? Domestic violence cut across all races, incomes and religious groups. "Sometimes calling the authorities is the kindest thing to do," he said as he rested his hand on the driver's door of the truck.

"But it would be against our *Ordnung.*"

"Still, it might force Wilmer into the kind of treatment he needs." Daniel wondered if he'd done the right thing by not calling the police himself. But he was an outsider, and if he interfered, Hannah might forbid Leah to see him again. His acceptance into this community was tenuous at best, and he didn't want to make things more difficult for Leah.

On the overseas missions, Daniel had watched his father tread the difficult path between doing what was right to prevent injustice and not interfering with the cultural practices of the host country. Daniel had believed he understood. Now he had an inkling of just how difficult his father's task had been. Daniel had always loved and admired him, as a teacher, a missionary and as a father. He only hoped he could do as well.

"What you did was very brave," Leah said.

Daniel shook his head. "I'm a man. Younger than Wilmer, and probably stronger. It's you who showed courage. You put yourself in danger to protect your sister."

She shrugged. "I had to. I couldn't let him hurt her."

Even now, hours after the incident, Daniel was still shaken by how close Leah had come to being harmed. The feeling of protectiveness that had swept over him, when he'd seen Wilmer shove her, had barely faded. Daniel wanted to draw her into the circle of his arms and hold her safe. Suddenly, keeping her from harm seemed like the most important thing in the world.

"Leah…" He broke off, unable to express his feelings.

She was gazing off into the distance. "This is such a difficult situation. I think Wilmer loves Johanna, no matter how he behaves."

"Maybe he does, but he shouldn't be anywhere near her."

"I agree, and so does my family. That includes Samuel. He's our deacon, and his opinion is important in a situation like this."

"What will happen if Wilmer refuses treatment? Will the bishop ignore it?"

"I don't think so. Bishop Atlee, our preachers and Samuel are good men, and they care about Johanna, as well as Wilmer. If he doesn't change, it's possible they could shun him."

"They still do that?"

She nodded. "They can. We don't look at it as punishment, but as an act of love—a last attempt to turn someone we care about from a terrible mistake. If Wilmer was shunned, no one would eat with him, talk to him or permit him in their homes."

"And your sister? Would she shun him as well?"

"She would. It would hurt her terribly, but Johanna's faith is strong. She wouldn't go against the bishop's ruling. And neither would Mam, at least not for Wilmer," Leah said.

"Let me make sure I understand this shunning." He met her gaze. "Your mother wouldn't turn against you if we married, would she?"

"Oh, no, Daniel. I haven't been baptized yet. It's my right to choose. It's only those who are full members of the church who can be shunned. At least in our community."

"If your bishop shunned Wilmer, would that include Johanna?"

"No. She and the children haven't done anything wrong. And if Wilmer was shunned, there's always a chance that he could redeem himself and then he could become one of us again."

"Good. That makes me feel a little better. I never like to see families separated, but it's better than what happened here today." He opened the vehicle door. "Can I see you tomorrow?"

She was so close that he could smell the shampoo in her hair and the scent of sunshine in her crisp Lincoln green dress and apron. She was so beautiful, his Leah. And for just a moment, uncertainty filled him. How could he think that a girl like her would leave her family and church for him? How could he be so arrogant to believe that he could be worthy of her?

"Tomorrow?" he repeated.

"I think I need to stay close, in case Mam or Johanna needs me," she said. "But you could come back after supper. We could walk down by the creek. It's pretty there, under the willow trees."

"If you need me before that, don't hesitate to call. You have my cell number." He knew that there was no phone at the farm, but he also knew the Yoders had phones available to them. "I'll come if you need me. Don't worry about the time. Day or night."

She laid her small hand over his, and a surge of warmth flowed up his arm. "I will call if I need you," Leah promised, "but we'll be fine. Bishop Atlee and the elders will take care of Wilmer." She removed her hand and smiled at him. "Your poor chin will be black and blue tomorrow and then you'll have to explain to your family what happened at our picnic dinner."

Daniel knew that he should start up his truck and go back to his aunt's house, but he didn't want to leave Leah. Not yet. "Would it be all right… Could we take that walk tonight?"

"I'd like that," she said, smiling up at him. "Stay here, while I tell Mam. I'm sure it will be okay."

Daniel got out of the pickup and leaned against it, waiting as Leah went back to the house. He wished he could talk to his dad, explain Johanna's situation and get his opinion, but it was too late to call. His parents rose early and were probably already in bed. Besides, talking to his father would mean also talking with his mother, and the last phone conversation he'd shared with her had centered on Leah.

His mother agreed with his aunt and uncle that marrying someone of the Amish faith would put a strain on the marriage from the start. "I'm sure she's a wonderful girl," his mother had said. "But it's so hard, as a young woman, to be in a strange country where you don't speak the language. You remember that your father and I married quickly so that he could accept a position in a mission overseas. I underestimated how difficult it would be. You don't know how many times I broke down and cried, how many times I wanted to leave our assignment and come home."

"You were younger than Leah, Mom. She'll be twenty-one in a few days."

"I was, but twenty-one is still young to go

so far from home and family. I was nineteen, stranded in an isolated village in Panama, alone when your dad had to travel. I felt so out of place that I doubted my own dedication to God's work. Nothing against your Leah, but you have to think of her happiness. You may be asking too much of her. If you marry in haste and the marriage fails, you could ruin her life as well as your own."

"Leah hasn't agreed to marry me yet, Mom," he'd answered. "And I've wrestled with every argument you can make against us marrying, but I can't get past the belief that we're meant to be together—that this is God's plan for us."

"Make certain you aren't confusing your own desire with that of the Lord's," she said, quietly. "Remember that we love you, and we'll support any decision you make—even if it's to marry a girl you haven't known more than a month."

His mother hadn't convinced him that Leah was wrong for him, but he knew that he hadn't convinced his mother that she was right for him, either. She would continue to worry and to give her advice, as she always had. His mom and Hannah Yoder would both be surprised to know they had that in common. Both mothers would rather see him and Leah part than marry.

Leah came toward him in the soft darkness. Daniel took his cell phone out of his pants pocket, turned off the power and tossed it on the front seat of the truck.

"I didn't bring a flashlight," she said, "but I could go back and get it—"

"No need," he said. "The moon is bright enough for us to find our way."

"Yes," she agreed. "It is, isn't it?" She caught his hand and led the way around the barn. Lantern light spilled through a small window. "Miriam's with Wilmer's horse," Leah said. "We think Wilmer drove him too hard and he fell on the road. His knees are a mess."

"I hate to see any animal mistreated."

"It just shows how sick Wilmer must be. He's not even able to care for his animals. Johanna brought the baby turkeys here the day after she came. We have them in the little shed off the utility room. You have to have a heat lamp if the temperature drops too low."

"Even in May?" He savored the feel of Leah's fingers clasped around his. *If we marry,* he thought, *I can hold her hand whenever I want.* A surge of joy rose in his chest. If Leah would only accept his offer of marriage, they'd share so much. He'd never know loneliness again.

"It can get cool on May nights," she said.

As they walked past the enclosed corral behind the barn, Daniel saw the white shapes of sheep. "I didn't know you had sheep," he said.

"Johanna's. She bought the original breeding pair with her quilt money. Wilmer never liked them, and she knew he wouldn't take care of them, so Uncle Reuben, Charley and Eli brought them here, too. A neighbor has been milking the cow for her."

"A shame she lives so far away."

"Yes, too far for Irwin to go back and forth to care for the animals twice a day. Last year, they rented a house at the end of our lane, the green farmhouse on the right. That was nice, to have her so close to all of us. But Wilmer's never satisfied. He's always looking for a better deal. They've moved four times since they were married."

"That's not a lot of moves," he said with a chuckle. "I can't tell you how many homes I've lived in."

"I've never moved. I was born in this house."

"My older brother and sister were born in Panama. I was born in Ohio. Matt in Oregon, and one of my younger sisters in Spain, the other one in South Dakota."

She glanced at him. "You lived in South Dakota?"

"I've lived a lot of places."

He'd thought that they would be talking about Johanna and her problems with Wilmer, but they didn't. Instead, they found themselves pouring out their hearts to each other. He told her about a Sunday school play he'd been in when he was four.

He'd been assigned the role of a shepherd who'd followed the star to Bethlehem and found the baby in the manger. He'd wanted to be Joseph, but that was a speaking part, reserved for an older boy. His brother was one of the three kings and wore a shiny crown. Somehow, when the time came for the shepherds and kings to make their grand entrance, Daniel found himself wearing the tinfoil crown on top of his washcloth headdress. The audience had howled with laughter, sending him wailing off stage, which pretty much ended his acting career.

Leah laughed heartily and quickly followed with an incident in her own childhood that had caused her much embarrassment in her later years. Soon they were so engaged in each other's stories that they were finishing each other's sentences and so much at ease that it seemed the most natural thing in the world was to find a mossy spot near a peach tree, sit down, lean back and stare up at the stars.

There were no airplanes overhead, and the sky was exceptionally clear. The stars shone so brightly that they seemed like glistening diamonds against a velvet blue-black heaven. Somehow, Leah's head was nestled against Daniel's shoulder and his arm was draped around her shoulders. It felt so good…so right.

"There's something I want to tell you," she said softly.

"You can tell me anything."

"Today, when Wilmer hit you and knocked you down, I was afraid for you, but more than that…" He heard her inhale deeply. "You were the strong one, Daniel. It's what I thought. That you were kind and strong and good. He hurt you, but you didn't get angry. You saw his pain and you just wanted to help him."

He didn't know what to say. It made him feel good that she thought he wasn't afraid, that he'd held to his nonviolent principles. But he hadn't had time to decide what to do. It was like that when he was treating someone with a medical emergency. He simply did what he had to and agonized over it later.

"I heard Him when you did that," Leah said. "Just as you told me that you hear Him. The Lord. Not with words in my ears, but in my heart. A feeling that it is right between us, that you have always been intended for me. And…" She hesitated and went on shyly. "And I realized then that I want you to court me, Daniel. I don't care what other people think—not even my family. I want to *walk out* with you, not to hide anymore, but to have everyone see us together. If you still want me?"

"I do," he said, tightening his arm around her. "I want it more than anything."

"Other than keeping your promise," she reminded him. "To God."

"Yes," he said. "But it seems to me that we can keep that promise together."

"I think so." She rose to her feet and took a few steps away from him. "We should get back," she said.

He got up and crossed the distance between them. She stood there, her heart-shaped face beautiful in the moonlight. As she took his hand, he couldn't help himself. He lowered his head and brushed her lips with his. For just an instant, she returned his kiss, and her lips were warm and soft and sweet.

"Oh, Daniel." She backed away from him. "That was nice."

"Yes," he said. "Better than nice."

"I think that means it's official," she said. "But you're supposed to ask me again."

"Ask you?" His stomach turned over. And his heart hammered in his chest.

She laughed, a joyous sound in the hushed darkness of the peach orchard. "To marry you, Daniel. You're supposed to ask me again."

"Will you do me the honor of becoming my wife, Leah Yoder?"

Laughing, she turned and darted away, her bonnet strings streaming behind her. "I'm thinking about it," she flung back over her shoulder.

He raced after her. For a few minutes, he was certain he'd catch her, but Leah was faster on her feet than he'd expected. And as he reached his pickup, she clattered up the back steps to the kitchen door. "Tomorrow," she called.

"I love you!" he shouted, not caring who heard. "I love you!"

With another peal of laughter, she flung open the door and went inside. Upstairs, a window opened and Susanna stuck her head out. She was giggling. "I love you, too!" Susanna shouted.

Red-faced and sweating but so happy that he was about to burst out of his skin, Daniel climbed into his truck. He turned around in the yard, stopped long enough to stare at the dark windows on the second floor, and finally drove away, whistling.

His aunt met him at the back door of her house. "Daniel! We've been trying to reach you. You've had a call from Pastor Bennett, from the committee. He wants you to contact him right away."

"He called *tonight*?" Daniel looked at his wrist

to check the time before remembering that he'd forgotten to put his watch on that morning. It was probably still lying on top of the dresser in his bedroom along with his wallet. "Is it too late to return his call?"

"No. John was adamant. He wants you to call him, no matter the time." She hugged him. "They've found a place for you! Wait until you hear where it is."

"He told you? Where is it? Do they want me to go back to Spain?" Usually, volunteers had several months to tie up their affairs in the States before going overseas. Unless the new post was in the United States. There'd been talk about an Indian reservation in New Mexico that might need help in their tribal clinic. Would his next assignment be in the Southwest? "Did Pastor Bennett say when I had to report to the mission? Will I be working in an established clinic?"

His aunt laughed and hugged him again. "I'm not telling. All I can say is that your uncle is very pleased. So am I, Daniel. We'll miss you terribly, but this will be such an adventure for you—a real chance to make a difference."

Uncle Allan was sitting at the kitchen table. "All things come to he who waits." He handed Daniel the wall phone. "Go ahead. Call Pastor Bennett."

Daniel was too nervous to sit. He found the

number, punched the buttons and held his breath as he heard the faint ring on the other end of the line. The pastor answered on the third ring. As pleasantries were exchanged, Daniel walked outside, onto the porch, to have a little privacy.

"We've had a bit of a scramble here," Pastor Bennett said in his deep, husky voice. "If you feel called to accept this responsibility, you're going to make a lot of people happy. Another family was scheduled to take the post. The wife was a nurse-practitioner, but one of their children was just diagnosed with juvenile diabetes, and they had to refuse the assignment since this is such a remote location."

"I'm sorry to hear that," Daniel said.

"As we all are. But you should know that two committee members submitted your name, Daniel. You're young, but we feel you're the right one to head up this mission."

"Head it up?" Daniel was certain he'd heard wrong. "I'm sorry, Pastor Bennett. Would you repeat that?"

"You heard me correctly, son. We're badly in need of an experienced RN with leadership qualities."

"I'm honored, but…" Suddenly he felt as if he couldn't get enough air in his lungs. He couldn't get his head around what John Bennett had said.

"I'm not ordained. I can't be in charge of the mission."

"Not necessary. We have three other families going. For one young couple, this will be their first mission. The other two families are old hands at this. We have several teachers, a farmer, a carpenter and an excellent pastor with twenty years of mission experience. We spoke with him, and he agreed that you would be a wonderful addition. And you should know that the committee voted unanimously to have you take charge."

"I'm speechless. I never expected…"

"You'll be setting up your own clinic. There isn't a medical facility for a hundred miles, and the population desperately needs your skills."

"My own clinic?"

"We have the funds for a small but fully supplied station. The post used to be a cattle ranch, but the jungle has reclaimed much of the pastureland. We've purchased some land on a navigable river to set up a school, a store and a self-sustaining farm. We also have a private donation to build a lovely church."

"Jungle? Did you say jungle? Pastor, where is this post?"

"Oh." Pastor Bennett laughed. "I thought your uncle and aunt would have told you. It's in the Amazon, Daniel. Brazil. Extremely remote. Your only electricity will be generator enabled, and the only practical way in or out is by boat or a float plane."

"But they speak Portuguese," Daniel reminded him. "I'm fluent in Spanish, not Portuguese."

"Not that important. Most of your patients will speak only one of a myriad of tribal dialects so interpreters who also speak Portuguese will be available. With a solid background in Spanish and your skill with languages, you'll soon make the switch to Portuguese. There is a locally trained woman with basic nursing skills who will act as your assistant. It's my understanding that she speaks both Portuguese and English."

Daniel tried to organize his thoughts. The Amazon? The area had always fascinated him. When he was a boy, he'd read every book he could find on the subject. "Would this be a two-year post?"

"Afraid not. The position is longer than usual because of the unique nature of this project. Starting from scratch, as it were. Your assignment will be for seven years."

Daniel felt light-headed. "Seven years?"

"Yes, but there're always opportunities to come back to the States on leave during that time."

Seven years? How could he ask Leah to leave her home and family for seven years? Daniel dropped into the porch swing.

"So what do you say? Do you feel up to this?"

Daniel was about to say *no*, that this had to be some mistake, that he wasn't qualified to take on such a challenge. But as he opened his mouth to refuse the post, he found himself thinking of the possibilities that stretched out in front of him. "I'd like to have a few days to consider…to pray for guidance," he said. "And there's…there's a young woman. I've asked her to be my wife. We just became engaged tonight, and she…" He trailed off.

"Good, good. Excellent. The only real issue is that the committee is hesitant to send a single man to head this project, especially one as young as yourself. But your engagement is the best news you could have given me. Tell your young woman that you're going to have to marry at once."

"And if I said yes…if she agreed, how long before we would leave?"

"We'd want you on location in thirty days, Daniel, so I'll need your answer within the week. A bit of a stretch, on both counts, I know, but we have faith you'll think this over and realize that when the Lord calls, sometimes we have to run to catch up with Him."

Chapter Sixteen

"The Amazon jungle? For seven years?" Leah stared at Daniel in disbelief as she tried to grasp what he was saying. "How is that possible?" A cold sensation coiled in the pit of her stomach and for a second, she felt light-headed.

Daniel had come back to the farm the following day, as he'd said he would, and she'd taken him down to the willows by the pond where they could be alone. When he'd gotten out of the truck, she'd sensed that something was wrong. His normally ruddy cheeks were pale, and his expression strained. She'd been afraid that he was coming down with something, or that he'd changed his mind about courting her, but she'd never expected to hear this.

"I didn't accept," Daniel said quickly. "I have a week to make my decision. Saying *yes* would mean that we'd have to marry within the next few weeks. The board can help with getting you a passport, but I have to go to Ohio to meet with the rest of mission group." He took her hand and squeezed it. "I'm as shocked as you are," he told her. "This isn't what I expected at all."

Leah swallowed, trying to dissolve the thickness in her throat. Daniel had waited so long for this assignment. She'd thought they might be getting a call to go to Spain or even back to Morocco, but the Amazon? Weren't there jaguars there? Giant snakes and alligators? She'd pictured herself in a city apartment or living in a tiny house on a busy street, but never in a jungle. "Seven years is a long time." She felt as if she might start weeping. Could she possibly leave her family for seven years?

"There are vacations," Daniel said. "There will be money for us to fly home, and we can always have visitors. We'll have our own home."

Leah's thoughts scattered in a hundred directions. "Could I have a garden?"

"A garden, a cow, whatever you like."

"But what would I do? Besides taking care of our house? I'm not a nurse. What help would I be in a jungle mission?" Leah turned her head away from him and stared at the pond. A mallard duck and her yellow and brown babies paddled by on the far side, the ducklings little more than balls of fluff. Home…all she'd ever known. How could Daniel ask her to leave this peaceful world to go to live in Brazil?

"There would be more work than hands to do it," he said in a burst of excitement. "The native population is sorely lacking medical attention. The infant mortality rate is high, nutrition is poor, the poverty overwhelming. Education is key in a place like this. We won't just be treating them medically, but we'll be helping them to help themselves. We can do so much to help them, to offer them a better way…to bring them to an understanding of God's love."

She looked at Daniel, still unable to speak.

"If you say you won't go, I'll turn them down," Daniel said.

"You have to let me think." She covered her face with her hands. "This is such a shock." So many questions surfaced in her mind and she groped for something sensible to say. "I took high school classes by mail. I got my diploma, and I wanted to teach in one of our Amish schools, but no position ever opened up. The elders won't allow college, but there was so much more that I wanted to learn. Do you think that would be possible? That I could continue studying by mail?"

"Not only by mail, but by computer. I'll need to be in contact with the nearest hospital, so we'll have satellite Internet. And the Internet would allow us to keep up with our families. Your mother and sisters could go to my aunt's house and use her computer. You could see them and talk to them, and they could see you."

Leah plucked a cloverleaf from the grass and tossed it on to the surface of the water. The breeze whirled it away. Like me, she thought, never to return. "So far away…" she murmured.

"I could refuse the post. I'm serious. I will if you say so. It won't be the only one offered."

Leah raised her head and looked into his eyes. "But how long before you're asked to be the leader again? These are special circumstances, Daniel."

"I don't have to be in charge. All I want to do is help people who are sick or injured. Being the leader of a mission is a heavy responsibility. It takes a rare person."

"If they chose you, they must think you are the best one for the job," Leah said.

"Maybe…I don't know." He pressed the heel of his hand to his forehead and then lowered it. "I only know that I don't want to go if it means losing you. I love you, Leah."

"And I love you," she said, gazing earnestly into his face. "But if it weren't for me, would you take this post?"

"I won't answer that…it isn't fair. You come first. You'll always come first in my life."

She shook her head. "No, be honest with me, Daniel. We've always said that God comes first, haven't we?"

"Yes, but… Maybe this is something *I* want. Maybe it's a test, not what God has planned for me, but a test to see—"

"No," she said firmly. "Either I'll marry you right away and we'll go to the Amazon together, or I won't marry you." She felt moisture well up in her eyes and spill over. "I have to decide. If I really love you, then where we go and what we do doesn't matter. I'd go with you with a willing heart."

"This is too much for me to ask of you. Too much too soon."

"With God and love on our side, nothing is too much," she answered. "I don't doubt *you*. It's *me*. It's been me all along. I'm not certain I'm strong enough to be the wife you deserve. I need time to think…to decide." She reached out and squeezed his hand. "Go home. When you're near me, I can't think of anything but you. Come back tomorrow afternoon, and I'll give you my answer then."

"Is it changing your faith to mine?" He rose and offered his hand to help her up. "Is that what troubles you?"

She shook her head, getting to her feet. "No, I think I could do that. It feels right. Maybe I was always meant to return to the church my mother was born in. Maybe that's my heritage, from all the Mennonites who came before her."

"If it's not that, then what—"

"Please, Daniel." She faced him. "If you really love me, you'll let me think this through." She took a deep breath. "Whatever I decide, I'll stick by. You have my word on that."

He went home as she asked...reluctantly, but he went.

After he was gone, Leah didn't return to the house. Instead she wandered through the meadow and into the peach orchard. She remembered the previous night so well... She could still feel the warmth of Daniel's lips on hers and the way it had made her feel. She hadn't felt wicked or daring, and she hadn't been ashamed of letting him kiss her. He was the first boy she'd ever kissed, and it had been worth waiting for. There was something about him so sweet and tender... so strong. How could it be wrong for them to be together as man and wife?

But doubt still tugged at her. She was certain Daniel would be a good husband and father, if the Lord saw fit to bless them with children. But was she worthy of him? Could she remain strong when the weeks, months and years stretched between her and her beloved family...when she'd broken the bond with her Amish faith? Or would she become weak and needy of his time and attention? Would she compromise Daniel's calling to serve as leader and medical caregiver for people who needed him so much?

She wanted to talk to Johanna…ask her opinion. Johanna knew her as well as Mam or any of her other sisters, and Johanna would be honest. If her sister thought she was too weak or might falter, she wouldn't hesitate to say so. And if Johanna believed that Leah had the strength, she would see past all the obstacles and urge her sister to follow her heart.

Leah started back for the house, walking fast, taking long strides. She'd find Johanna and pull her aside where she could spill out her heart. Leah knew what she wanted, but she needed to hear Johanna say it. But when she reached the farmyard, she stopped short and stared.

Bishop Atlee's buggy was there, and so was Samuel's. A red-faced Irwin stood stock-still by the windmill with a bucket of chicken feed in each hand and tears running down his face. As Leah tried to think what could be wrong, she saw Eli running up the lane.

Something was terribly wrong. Someone was dead. "Mam!" Leah cried as she broke into a run.

Susanna sat on the back step, her face in her hands, weeping.

"What's happened?" Leah cried as a terrible feeling of dread washed over her. "Is it Mam?" Not her mother or one of her sisters! Not Johanna's baby or little Jonah! Not Charley, with his laughing ways and easy manner of taking charge! "Aunt Jezzy?"

Susanna raised her head. She was sobbing so hard that she could barely speak. "Johanna," she managed. "Johanna's…" She began gasping and hiccupping.

Leah dashed past her and flung open the kitchen door. "Johanna!"

But there was Johanna sitting stone-faced and dry-eyed at the table with both children in her arms, and there was Mam standing behind her, her complexion pale with shock. Leah searched the room with her gaze, counting off those who were dearest to her: Anna, Ruth, Miriam, Rebecca. *Grossmama* sat in the rocker, face pinched, mouth tight. Charley stood behind Miriam, his hand on her shoulder. Anna wasn't crying, so it couldn't be one of Samuel's children who'd come to misfortune.

"What is it?" Leah asked. Familiar faces turned toward her.

Anna caught her hand and drew her aside. "Wilmer," she whispered. She shook her head. "God rest his soul."

Leah didn't understand. "What did he do?

He didn't try to hurt Johanna or the children, did he?"

Anna's eyes were kind as she tugged Leah back out onto the porch. "My Samuel found him. Wilmer was staying with the bishop until his brother could come from Ohio to take him back there, but last night, he climbed out a window. They looked for him everywhere at the Atlees'. They thought it better not to say anything until they found him. But Samuel, he had a hunch. He went back to the farm and searched. He found him in the corncrib. He had taken his own life, probably last night." Anna eyes brimmed with compassion. "So awful for Johanna and the children."

"Poor Johanna," Leah choked out. "How is she?"

"You know our Johanna. Strong. She hasn't cried, not one tear, but I know she weeps here." Anna touched the spot over her heart.

"I am so sorry."

"Ya," Anna murmured. "We all are. He was very troubled, Wilmer. Maybe so sick that God will not hold him responsible for what he's done." She squeezed Leah's hand. "We will pray for him."

"And for Johanna and the children."

"Ya, for Bishop Atlee as well. He is such a

good man, and now he will feel responsible that he tried to help Wilmer and couldn't."

Just what Daniel said, Leah thought. *We should have listened to Daniel and called the police. If we had, Wilmer might still be alive.*

"And your Samuel," she said to her sister. "Poor Samuel."

Anna bit her lower lip and nodded. "Better it was him than Johanna or one of the children." Then she opened her arms, and Leah went into her embrace and they cried tears of regret together.

Leah walked across the field and crossed the road to the chair shop. A *Closed* sign hung in the window; normally, the business would have been open until six on a weekday, but Roman had closed early. She'd passed him and Fannie on their way to Mam's, so no one was at home there but the children, and they would be in the house or the barnyard. At the shop, she retrieved the key from a nail under the porch and let herself inside the salesroom.

She had to talk to Daniel; Wilmer's death changed everything. She couldn't wait for Daniel to come tomorrow for her answer. She had to see him face-to-face, as soon as possible. She went behind the counter where a black phone hung on the wall. Hands damp with moisture, Leah punched in the number for Daniel's cell phone, and when he answered, she asked him to come.

"What's is it, Leah? Have you been crying?" Daniel asked.

"Just come to the chair shop. Come now," she said before hanging up the phone.

Too agitated to sit, she folded her arms and paced up and down the large room. Daniel would understand what she had to do. It would break both of their hearts, but there was no other way. Leaving her family now, when they needed her most—when Johanna needed her most—was impossible. Daniel would understand. And maybe it would be easier this way. Now, she didn't have to make a decision. The decision had been made for her.

The church would come together to support Johanna and her children in her time of grief. Neighbors would arrange for any work that had to be done at her farm, there would be food to feed all those who would come to offer condolences, and later attend the funeral. Considering the manner of Wilmer's passing, there was no way to keep the authorities from getting involved, but when they were finished, and Wilmer's body had been prepared for burial, he would be laid out in Mam's parlor.

Johanna would sew white trousers and a shirt for Wilmer to be buried in, and the men would

place him in a simple pine coffin. Johanna and
the family would sit up all night, keeping vigil
and praying. The house would be full of visitors until the third day, when the preachers
would offer a final service for the deceased and
a procession of buggies would file slowly to the
Graabhof—the Amish cemetery.

The church and the Amish community would
unite to help Johanna, but it would be her family
that she would need most. Ruth and Miriam
and Anna lived nearby, but they had husbands
and responsibilities of their own. Leah was the
eldest daughter still at home. Supporting Johanna
would fall on her shoulders, and it would be impossible to let down those who counted on her.
She could no more go off to the jungles of Brazil
with Daniel than she could fly off a roof.

The sound of truck tires on gravel tore Leah
from her thoughts, and she went out on the porch
and down the steps. Daniel got out of the truck
and hurried toward her. Each step she took felt
as if her shoes were made of concrete, but she
forced herself to be brave. She could not be selfish and think of her own happiness. She had to
think of Johanna.

"Daniel…" A lump rose in her throat. She
would not cry. If she cried, she might not get
through what she had to say.

"Leah, I'm so sorry. I just heard about your

sister's husband. My uncle's a volunteer on the fire department and he called my aunt as I was going out the door."

He put out his arms, but she stepped away and shook her head.

"I can't marry you, Daniel. I'm sorry, but I can't."

"You're upset," he argued. "We don't need to talk about this now."

"Follow your dream," she said. "Find someone who will be the wife and helpmate you need. But it can't be me."

"I'll tell them *no.* I'll stay here, Leah—here in Kent County. Maybe, in time—"

She shook her head again. "I can't leave my family. Not now, not ever. I was wrong to let you think I could."

"But, Leah—"

"I need you to go, Daniel." Dry-eyed but weeping inside, she turned and walked back into the chair shop, locked the door behind her and pulled down the blind.

He followed her to the door and banged and called her name, but she didn't answer. It would be better this way, she told herself, better for her family and better for Daniel. In time, he'd understand that she was right. And the quicker she freed him to go, the kinder it would be for both of them.

"Just let me talk to you," he begged.

It pained her to hear him crying, but she didn't answer. And finally, after nearly an hour, she heard his footsteps on the steps and the crunch of gravel. The truck door shut, the engine roared to life and Daniel drove out of her life.

Chapter Seventeen

Back home, the house was teeming with people. Mam, Susanna and Johanna sat in the parlor while friends and neighbors offered condolences and promised to offer prayers for Wilmer. Lydia and Fannie were there, as well as Wilmer's sister and Aunt Martha. For once, Aunt Martha had nothing critical to say. She'd hugged Johanna, offered to help in any way she could and took baby Katy to Rebecca and Dorcas in the backyard.

Leah asked Mam what she should do first. In moments, she and Ruth were laying white material out on the floor in the upstairs hall. Ruth went up to the attic and came down with an old suitcase. In it was a pattern that Mam had used to make their father's funeral clothes, and they used that to pin and cut the garments that Johanna would need to sew for Wilmer.

Leah tried not to think about Daniel, about

what she'd said to him, about how she'd hurt him.
She hoped he wouldn't hate her, and she wished
there had been some other way to send him
away. She felt empty inside, as cold and black
as a fireplace when the last coals have gone out
and the winter wind blew down the chimney.
She told herself that she'd done the right thing,
the only thing. Only a selfish woman would
have put her own happiness ahead of her sister's
need. This was where she belonged…where God
wanted her.

She was busy through supper and afterwards.
It wasn't until after Katy and Jonah had been
tucked into bed with Mam, and an exhausted
Johanna had retired to her room, that Leah had
time to think. Anna, Ruth and Miriam had gone
home, promising to come back first thing in
the morning. Samuel had taken the last load of
Grossmama's things to his house. The neighbors had left, and only Rebecca, Irwin and Aunt
Jezebel remained at the kitchen table talking and
eating slices of a pie that Anna had baked.

But Leah didn't want to join them. She didn't
want to talk to anyone, and she didn't want pie.
She didn't care if she ever ate again. She wanted
to be alone, but she could think of no place in the
house that didn't have someone sleeping there.
Even the parlor was taken. Wilmer's sister refused to stay at his house, and Mam had gotten

Miriam and Irwin to make up a borrowed air mattress in the parlor for her. Leah thought of going outside, maybe to sit on the porch and look at the stars, but that would mean going through the kitchen, and Rebecca would want to know why she was going outside at ten o'clock at night. And worse, she might ask why Daniel hadn't come to offer his condolences.

Instead, Leah found matches in a hall closet, lit a kerosene lantern and carried it up two flights of stairs to the attic. The third story had once been used as bedrooms; now it was just storage. And like the rest of the house, Mam believed in keeping it free of dust and cobwebs. When she was small, Leah had loved to come up here with her sisters to play games on rainy days. The rooms on either end of the attic had exposed brick chimneys. No fireplaces or stoves, but the heat from the downstairs warmed the bricks and made the space cozy, even on a damp and windy day. The room on the west end held furniture not needed downstairs, and it was to this retreat that Leah fled and finally let the tears fall.

She wasn't sure how long she'd been there when she heard footsteps on the bare wood floors. For just an instant, *Grossmama*'s ghost stories surfaced in her mind and gooseflesh rose on the back of her neck. But then, her own good sense took over, and she called out, "Who's there?" A shadowy figure appeared and Leah's breath caught in her throat. "Who—"

"Child, child, whatever are you doing up here all by yourself?"

"Aunt Jezzy?"

"I wondered who'd found my secret spot. Why, Leah, sweet, you've been crying." Aunt Jezebel sat down beside her on the day bed mattress. "Weeping for poor lost Wilmer or your sister?"

Leah tried to answer, but found herself sobbing uncontrollably. Aunt Jezzy put her arms around her and pulled her against her soft bosom. "There, there, child. It will be all right. It will. God's in his heaven, and Wilmer's in a better place. As bad as things look right now, Johanna will be happy again someday. I promise you that."

"Ne...ne." Another round of sobbing followed. "It's...it's me I cry for," Leah wailed. "Oh, Aunt Jezzy, I sent Daniel away. He wanted to marry me...and now I'll never see him again."

"Shh, shh." Her great aunt patted Leah's back. "Sent him away? But I thought you loved him."

"I did...I do, but now..." The words tumbled out, one after another, and by the time Leah had finished explaining why she'd had to do what she'd done, her storm of tears had passed.

The older woman fumbled in her apron pocket and produced a clean, white handkerchief.

"Blow," she ordered, handing Leah the handkerchief. Leah did as she was told. "We all thought you were going to marry him and turn Mennonite," Aunt Jezzy said. "Even Hannah thought so."

"I was," Leah said faintly. "But after what's happened…Johanna needs me. Mam needs me. It would be wrong to go and leave them in the midst of all this trouble."

"Wrong, is it?"

"And selfish to want to go," Leah said.

Her great aunt shook her head. "Child, I don't believe that. You don't have a selfish bone in your body. I saw how you looked after Levina when she broke her hip. She's not an easy person, and she has a sharp tongue, but you persevered. She's my sister and your grandmother, but there are times, I can tell you, I've wished her at the far end of the country from me. So, don't tell me you're selfish. *Ne,* I won't accept that."

Leah sniffed. "I'm sure staying home…I'm sure it's what God would want me to do."

Aunt Jezebel arched one graying eyebrow. "Certain, are you?"

"I think so." Leah nodded. "Yes, I'm certain of it."

"Well, I think you're wrong." She used the corner of her apron to wipe a tear off Leah's cheek. "Listen to me, child. I wasn't always a withered old woman that some people call touched in the head. I had a beau, a poor boy without a horse or a buggy or an acre to his name, but I loved him. My mother and father were set against him, and so I refused his offer of marriage and sent him away."

"And you were sorry afterwards?"

"Sorry every day of my life," Aunt Jezzy said. "He married someone else, had children, worked hard, made a good life. She was happy, his wife. It could have been me if I'd had the courage to follow my heart instead of listening to other folks."

"It's why you never married."

"Never found anyone else who held a candle to him. Didn't want second best. Maybe I'm a one-man woman, a foolish one, but faithful. You see, Leah, I think God sent Benjamin to me, hard though the road might have been, and I turned my back on him." She pursed her lips. "Why do I think you're making the same mistake?"

"But Johanna needs me."

"Johanna would want you to be happy, Leah. She would want you to find a good man, to marry him and to live the best life you can. You're not indispensible. Johanna has a circle of family here to help her. Have you thought that you might be using Johanna's sorrow as an excuse to keep you from taking a leap of faith?"

* * *

They slept there, the two of them, on that daybed in the attic…or rather Aunt Jezzy slept. Leah lay awake, dry eyed, praying and thinking. And when the first rays of dawn spread coral feathers of light across the sky in the east, she crept down the stairs and out to the barn.

She was harnessing Blackie to Dat's buggy when Miriam came into the stable to start the morning milking. "Coming in late or going out early?" her sister asked.

"I'm going to Daniel," Leah said. Her voice was husky from lack of sleep, but she wasn't a bit tired. "I made a mistake. I turned down his offer of marriage, but I've changed my mind. I'm going to marry him if he'll still have me."

Miriam frowned. "I was afraid of that."

"Don't be angry with me. It feels right," Leah said. "Daniel feels right to me. I think this is what was always meant to happen…for one of us to go back to the faith Mam left for Dat."

Miriam nodded. "I'll take the rails down. It hasn't rained in days. You'll make better time if you cut across the pasture, let yourself out of the woods' gate and follow the logging trail to the road beyond Samuel's."

"Tell Mam and the others where I've gone."

"I will." She stepped close and touched Leah's

cheek. "It wouldn't be my choice, but maybe it is the right one for you. Daniel's a good man."

"I think Dat would have liked him."

Miriam chuckled and began to check the straps on the gelding's harness. "I think Dat would have run him off this farm with a pitchfork. Go with God, little sister. And mind Blackie. He's full of ginger this morning."

Miriam was right about Blackie. By the time they reached the hard road, the horse was eager to go. He started off at a smooth trot, his shod hooves flying over the pavement. But Leah didn't care. This was one time that she wanted Blackie to go as fast as he could. She had to get to Daniel and tell him how foolish she'd been.

But when she pulled into the driveway of Joyce and Allan's house, the first thing Leah saw was the empty spot where Daniel always parked his truck. *He's gone,* she thought. *I'm too late. I've really lost him.* She didn't cry; there were no tears left. She was turning Blackie around in the yard when Daniel's aunt came out the back door and saw her.

"Leah? What are you doing here?"

Leah stared at her, numbly. How could she explain what she'd done? How wrong she'd been? "I was looking for Daniel," she called raggedly.

"You just missed him. He has a flight out of

Baltimore." Joyce approached the buggy. "He loves you, Leah. I'm so sorry about your sister, and sorry that the two of you couldn't…" She broke off, obviously choked up with emotion. "I know I wasn't as welcoming as I should have been. It's just that we think of Daniel as our own son, and we didn't want to see him hurt."

"I understand," Leah said, turning the reins in her hands. "My mother was against it, too. She was afraid that we…that it wouldn't…"

"I was wrong," Joyce said. "When we saw how Daniel was last night, Allan and I realized that we should have been more supportive. We want you to know that you're always welcome in our home and at our worship services."

"Thank you," Leah said, looking out into the barnyard. "He's really gone?"

"Yes." Joyce nodded. "I'd offer to call him for you, to see if I could get him to turn around and come back, but he left his cell phone in the bathroom. You know how he is. That boy would leave his head if it wasn't attached."

Leah nodded. "I know how he is." *How he was,* she thought. Aunt Jezebel was right. She had been so busy trying to guess what God wanted her to do that she hadn't been listening to His answer. He'd sent her a wonderful man to be her husband, and she'd sent him away because she was too scared to put her trust in Him. She lowered her head and then looked up again. "I'm sorry to bother you. I guess I'll just go home."

"No bother at all. Tell your sister how sorry we are. Some of us from the church will be bringing over food next week. I'm sure you're well stocked now. And we'd like to come by and pay our respects, if that's all right."

"Yes," Leah said. "Johanna would like that, I'm sure." She waved to Joyce and turned Blackie's head down the drive. Her great aunt's words echoed in her head. *"Sorry every day of my life…"* Moisture clouded her vision and she blinked away hot salt tears. "Oh, Daniel, I'm so sorry," she whispered. "So sorry."

Suddenly, Blackie came to an abrupt halt, planted all four feet and reared in the traces. At the same instant, the pickup truck that had turned into the drive screeched to a stop, tires sliding in the gravel, and Daniel flung himself out of the driver's door.

"Leah!"

"Daniel!"

She pulled hard on the reins, and when the buggy stopped rocking, she jumped down and ran to catch hold of Blackie's bridle. Daniel rushed toward her, and together they settled the horse. Somehow in the excitement, Daniel's aunt and uncle had come out of the house.

"Let me hold that horse," Allan said.

"Thank you," Leah and Daniel said at the same time.

Daniel caught hold of Leah's arm and pulled her around to the back of the house and into the relative seclusion of the grape arbor. "You're here," he said. "I thought... You told me... But you're here."

She was breathless, giddy. Her knees felt weak. "You left," she managed. "You left for the airport."

"I forgot my ticket."

Leah began to laugh. "And your cell phone."

"My phone, too?" He pulled her into his arms. "Tell me that I'm not dreaming. That you're really here? That you've changed your mind?"

"You're not dreaming," she murmured. "I'm here, and I changed my mind."

"Why? Why would you ever want to be with such a dunce who can't even get to the airport with all his belongings?"

"Hush," she said, slipping her arms around his neck and raising on her tiptoes to kiss him. "Because I love you and want to marry you."

"Really?"

"Daniel Brown, will you quit talking and kiss me?"

And when he finally did kiss her, there was no need for them to say anything else at all.

Epilogue

*Amazon Rain Forest—Eighteen Months
Later...*

"Wake up, wife." Daniel kissed the tip of Leah's
nose.

She stirred, snuggled down deeper into her
bed and pulled the pillow over her head. Daniel
sat on the mattress beside her and bounced.

"Mmm," Leah murmured. "Just a little longer."

Daniel laughed. "Open your eyes, darling. I
have a surprise for you."

Groaning, she pulled the pillow aside and
peeked up at him. Daniel waved a thick brown
envelope in front of her nose.

"Mail? Really?" She flung the pillow back and
sat up, reaching for the packet. "For me?"

Still chuckling, he waved the envelope just out
of her reach. "A boat arrived this morning with
supplies, books, your new sewing machine and

what looks like six months of the *Budget,* all addressed to Mrs. Daniel Brown, Bethesda Mission. I suppose that must be you."

Leah flung aside the sheet. "Give me my letters, please." Excitement thrummed through her, sending ribbons of joy to the tips of her toes.

"Breakfast first," Daniel said. "Midwife's orders. Caridade came by with a ripe pineapple, a bowl of figs and mangos, and a pitcher of fresh-squeezed orange juice. Nothing too good for *little teacher in the family way.*"

Leah wiggled out from under the sheet, pushed aside the mosquito netting and slid to the floor. Daniel handed her a white organdy duster to cover her modest white cotton nightgown and shook out each of her soft leather huaraches to make certain no spiders were hiding there before slipping them onto her feet.

"How's the tummy?"

Leah took a deep breath and smiled at him. "Good." She quickly pinned up her braids, took her small, lacy Mennonite prayer *kapp* off the nightstand, and fastened it on the back of her head. "Really good. I think I'm hungry." She was only three months along, and had had morning sickness for weeks, but it seemed to be passing.

He laughed. "It's about time. I made you breakfast—fig and Brazil nut muffins and a soft-boiled egg."

"Mmm, sounds delicious, but I'd rather have my letters first, then eat."

Daniel shook his head and chuckled. "Oh, no. First the egg—"

"One bite?" she bargained as she followed him through the tiny thatched-roofed cottage. Out on the covered porch, Daniel had set the breakfast table for two, complete with fresh-cut pink orchids floating in a hand-thrown pottery bowl and a basket of fruit.

As she sat down, she looked around her, marveling at the beauty of the Amazon rain forest and the slow-moving river that bordered the clearing. "This must be what the Garden of Eden looked like," she said as she drank in the wonder of the soaring capirone, capok and leafy cercropia trees that sheltered her jungle home.

"You say that every morning," he teased as he took his chair.

"It's true, isn't it?" As she watched, a scarlet macaw took flight from a lower branch of a Brazil nut tree, his colorful feathers a slash of brilliance against the green backdrop of the jungle. "You've brought me to paradise."

"Not every wife would think that." He chuckled as he poured her a brimming glass of orange juice. "No running water, electricity only a few hours a day, no grocery stores or shopping malls."

"But bananas and lemons grow in our backyard." She held out her hand. "My letters from home?"

"Actually, you might want to wait on the letters." He looked over his shoulder again. "There's another surprise. Why don't you have some egg while we wait?"

"Another surprise?" She gazed into his handsome face. *I couldn't have found a more devoted husband, not if I'd searched the world over,* she thought. And the chasm she'd thought she was crossing—from the Amish faith to the Mennonite faith, had turned out to be only a series of slow, easy steps. Now, to her joy, they were expecting a child who she hoped might inherit Daniel's beautiful green eyes and his loving spirit. "How can I eat when you tell me you have another surprise?"

"You need to eat for the baby."

Leah started to argue, then bowed her head and closed her eyes for grace. Daniel Brown could be a stubborn man, she'd learned; sometimes it was just easier to play along with him.

"Thanks be to the Lord for all His blessings," Daniel said. "And for you, who left so much behind for me."

She opened her eyes and smiled at him. "I do miss my family," she said, "but there's so much to do here. My preschool and Sunday School classes, and the sewing circle with the women."

She remembered that Daniel had said the new sewing machine had come on the boat. That would make her sewing group's fledgling enterprise so much easier. Many of the young women who had come to live near the mission were single mothers or widows without education and no means to support their children. Leah had proposed that they start a business making a high-quality line of baby clothing that could be sold at Mennonite-owned stores and bazaars in the United States. They'd begun the project only eight months ago, and already they were showing a profit, with a potential for selling as many garments as the women could produce.

"When the baby's old enough to travel, we'll go home on leave," Daniel assured her. "Three months. And you'll get to show off Rachel to your mother and sisters."

"Or David," she teased. "I think this is going to be a boy."

"Boy or girl, I'll be happy with, either." He slid a muffin, sliced banana and a small bowl with the soft-boiled egg onto her plate.

"You spoil me, Daniel."

"You deserve to be spoiled," he answered.

Leah nibbled at the egg. Surprisingly, she found it delicious and devoured every bite of the egg, the banana and half a muffin before taking a swallow of orange juice. "Now, what's the other surprise," she asked.

Mischief sparkled in Daniel's eyes.

"Is it a monkey?" Leah clasped her hands. "You've found me a baby squirrel monkey?" One of the women who attended her sewing circle had a pet squirrel monkey with a pretty little white face and a brown cap of fur that Leah had found adorable. Orphan monkeys were sometimes brought to the mission, and Daniel had been promising that the next time one appeared, she could have it.

"No," he said. "Better than a monkey."

"Not a sloth." She wrinkled her nose. "I don't want a sloth." Daniel had argued that a sloth would be a lot less trouble than a monkey with the baby coming.

"You'll like this, I promise. Close your eyes." He rose, stepped behind her, and covered her eyes with his hands.

"Hurry," Leah said impatiently. Then she heard footsteps on the porch.

"Surprise," Daniel said, as he dropped his hands.

Leah stared, not certain she could believe her eyes. Standing there on her porch were Miriam and Charley. "Miriam!" she cried, leaping out of her chair. "Charley! Am I dreaming?"

And then they were all laughing and hugging

each other, and Leah was crying for joy. "How?" she demanded. "How did you get here?"

"It was Susanna's idea," Miriam said between hugs. "She said she missed you and we should come to see if you were all right. Everyone in Seven Poplars agreed it was time someone looked in on you two, so everyone contributed a little to pay for the plane tickets. Even Aunt Martha." She chuckled.

"Even Aunt Martha?" Tears filled Leah's eyes. She knew her pregnancy was making her emotional, but she was truly touched that Aunt Martha, who had little money, would contribute to Charley and Miriam's trip. "Does that mean she's forgiven me for marrying Daniel, leaving the church and moving to South America?"

"No one at home is angry with you, silly goose." Miriam hugged her sister again. "You're serving God here, just in a different way than we do."

"How long can you stay?" Leah demanded, squeezing Miriam's hands in hers. "A long time, I hope."

"Through Christmas." Miriam grinned. "Almost three weeks. So you won't be alone for Christmas."

"I couldn't ask for a better Christmas gift." Leah looked at Daniel. "Did you know they were coming?"

He nodded. "Just for a few weeks. I thought that since you'd been feeling under the weather, this would cheer you up."

Miriam looked back to Leah, her face falling. "You're not sick, are you?"

"Nothing that another six or seven months won't cure," Daniel teased.

Blushing, Leah turned and pressed her face into her husband's chest and his strong arms drew her in to a warm embrace. "You shouldn't say that," she whispered. "Not in front of Charley."

"Why not?" Charley asked. "We're all family, aren't we?"

"Ya," Miriam said, clasping Charley's hand. "We're all family. Even if some of us do wear smaller *kapps*."

* * * * *

Dear Reader,

If you're returning to the Yoder farm for another visit, welcome back! If this is your first time with us, I'm so glad you could join us around Hannah's cozy kitchen table. It's springtime in Seven Poplars, everyone is busy turning the soil, planting seeds and picking strawberries, but we always have room for one more. Here in Seven Poplars, the sun is bright, the grass is sweet-smelling and love is in the air. Hannah's daughter, Leah, has always been different than the others, always looking out the window while the other girls were looking in. When Leah meets the Mennonite missionary, Daniel, his presence not only has the potential to affect her life, but the lives of every member of the Yoder family. What do you do when you fall in love with an outsider? And if the larger world beckons, is it temptation or simply another of life's doorways?

I hope you enjoy your time with Leah and Daniel and that their story brings as much pleasure to you in reading it, as it has me in writing it. I found Leah, in many ways, to be different than her sisters. She's so worldly! And yet there's an innocence about her that makes me smile.

Next time we get together, I have a special surprise for you! A secret visitor, lost to the Amish world and in desperate need of love and understanding. Can Hannah welcome this young woman into her arms? Will the Yoder household ever be the same again?

Wishing you peace and joy,
Emma Miller

Questions for Discussion

1. Do you think it was a good idea for the bishop to allow the Gleaners youth group to go to the Mennonite program?

2. Once Leah realized she was interested in Daniel, could she have kept herself from falling in love with him if she had stopped seeing him? Do you think Hannah should have advised her daughter to avoid Daniel?

3. Do you think Daniel decided too quickly that he was in love with Leah and wanted to marry her? Do you believe in love at first sight? Do you think it's possible that God put Leah in Daniel's path?

4. At one point, Susanna says she wants to marry Samuel, and Leah teases her about Samuel already being married. Do you think it was okay for Leah to lead her sister to believe that she could, perhaps, marry some day? Considering Susanna's mental challenges, would it have been kinder for Leah to explain to Susanna that she would always remain at home with their mother?

5. Were you surprised to learn that Wilmer, an Amish man, was suffering from depression? Have you ever known anyone suffering from depression? How did you deal with it in your life? Do you think that Wilmer's story might have ended differently if he had sought professional help?

6. Leah kept saying that her outings with Daniel weren't dates. Was that true? By Amish standards? By English standards? Do you think that Leah was trying to convince Daniel or herself that the two of them weren't *walking out* together?

7. Do you think that if Daniel's aunt and uncle had been stronger in discouraging the relationship between Daniel and Leah, that Daniel might not have pursued Leah? Were you surprised that Daniel's family was worried about the possible relationship?

8. At what point do you think Mam realized something was going on between Daniel and Leah? Should she have said something to Leah then? If she had forbidden Leah to see Daniel again, do you think Leah would have obeyed?

9. Did Leah do the right thing in leaving her family to go with Daniel? Why or why not? Have you ever been forced to make this kind of decision? How did you decide what was best? And if Leah hadn't met Daniel, do you think she would have been happy living as a member of the Old Order Amish Church? Do you feel that she compromised her faith in becoming Mennonite?

LARGER-PRINT BOOKS!

**GET 2 FREE
LARGER-PRINT NOVELS
PLUS 2 FREE
MYSTERY GIFTS**

Love Inspired

Larger-print novels are now available...

LILP11B

Love Inspired®
SUSPENSE
RIVETING INSPIRATIONAL ROMANCE

Watch for our series of edge-
of-your-seat suspense novels.
These contemporary tales
of intrigue and romance
feature Christian characters
facing challenges to their faith...
and their lives!

AVAILABLE IN REGULAR
& LARGER-PRINT FORMATS

For exciting stories that reflect traditional values,
visit:
www.ReaderService.com